the Clovis Caper

JANE TRAHEY, a native of Chicago, is a graduate of Mundelein College and holds a master's degree from Columbia University. She has been Advertising Director for Neiman-Marcus in Dallas and president of her own advertising agency. She is also the author of several books for adults and young people, including *Life with Mother Superior*, which became the movie *The Trouble with Angels*. Jane Trahey divides her time between Chicago and New York City.

the Clovis Caper

Jane Trahey

AN AVON CAMELOT BOOK

THE CLOVIS CAPER is an original publication of Avon Books. This work has never before appeared in book form.

AVON BOOKS
A division of
The Hearst Corporation
105 Madison Avenue
New York, New York 10016

First Avon Camelot Printing: March 1990

CAMELOT TRADEMARK REG. U.S. PAT. OFF. AND IN OTHER COUNTRIES, MARCA REGISTRADA, HECHO EN U.S.A.

Printed in the U.S.A.

OPM   10   9   8   7   6   5   4   3   2   1

for Clovis

Chapter 1

Martin Prentiss was soaked. He could hear his waterproof docksiders squish as he sloshed along the fifteenth floor of the William James building for his appointment with Dr. Griffin. He heard the Memorial Church bong its sharp four o'clock bells and checked his watch. No point in being early. He turned the brass knob on the door and slipped in. Dr. Griffin was sitting by the window reading his Wall Street *Journal*. He looked up as Martin dropped his drenched jacket on the floor by the door.

Martin knew that first Dr. Griffin would stand up and bow him into his chair just as a headwaiter would. "And how are you on this beautiful day?"

Dr. Griffin pushed Martin's chair toward his desk. It was a scene they played every day. Martin scraped up a smile for the doctor. His eyes followed the tall, graying, slightly pudgy man around his desk. He watched him dump his newspaper in the out basket. Dr. Griffin dragged his desk chair out and, grunting, slid into it. Martin knew that he overplayed the grunts.

"I'll tell you one thing, Martin," he sighed. "If you

want to force the price of a stock down, just let Phil Griffin buy it.''

Martin waited for the doctor to pull out his box of candy and offer Martin a piece from the shiny display. Martin shook his head. He didn't like candy anymore. He thought about this. He used to love Hershey bars but now everything, especially chocolate, stuck in his throat.

He watched the doctor's index finger scan the top layer of the box for his favorite piece. When he spied a nougat, his hand was like a missile heading for its target. Whaaam! Dr. Griffin picked it up and popped it in his mouth and grinned. "Wonnerful, jus' wonnerful." He chewed happily. "Sure you don't want some?"

Then he beaded in for more target practice. Zooming in for another piece, he pinched the bottoms of the chocolates. "Pink!" he said disgustedly. "I hate pinks." The lemon yellow cream was also a loser. Both pieces hit the trash can. Martin admired Dr. Griffin's surefire hits into the wastebasket. He never missed.

Martin's eyes were glued on Dr. Griffin. He really liked him and wished to heaven that he had something to say that would make the doctor happy. He didn't. He'd known the doctor for as long as he could remember. He was *his* godfather and his dad's best friend. The two of them socked tennis balls every other night and once a week they had dinner on the town. His mom had called their weekly outing "Junk Food Night." Dad used to coax her to come along but she wouldn't budge.

"No, you fellows should have a night all on your own to bore each other with Harvard department intrigue. Martin and I are eating at the Ritz."

Funny, it was really the other way around. He and his mom would race off to the Junk Food King and eat baby hamburgers with extra pickles and drink jumbo shakes. It was Dad and Uncle Phil who went to the Ritz. He saw that

2

Dr. Griffin's lips were moving but he didn't hear any words. He tried to pay attention.

He watched the doctor tuck the candy box away and pull out an envelope from the stack of papers. Martin recognized his report card. His dad must have brought it to Dr. Griffin this morning. He'd watched his dad scan the card at breakfast. He hadn't said a thing about it, just tucked it into his jacket pocket, come around the table, and given him a hug. He'd rubbed his cheek up against Martin's and said, "Love you, you know."

Martin just loved the way his dad smelled. It was his scented soap. His mom had said no one was kookier than his dad on the subject of soap. It had to be fern-scented. It came from a special shop on Charles Street.

Dr. Griffin held the report card toward him. He could see his straight D record. "Well," said the doctor, "you didn't come here to talk about my investments. But I'll tell you this, Martin, you keep this up and you won't ever *have* to worry about investments. You won't have anything to invest. How's the cassette?"

Martin heard this last jarring sentence. He wished to heaven he'd never mentioned the tape to Dr. Griffin.

"You still playing it?"

Martin nodded.

"It still makes you unhappy. But you keep on playing it?"

Martin knew that Dr. Griffin would never understand that the tape of his mom made him happy as well as making him sad. The doctor had scolded him and asked, "Why don't you just erase the stuff that gets to you and leave the good parts on?"

Martin couldn't tell him that he could rewind the tape and fast-forward it. But there was no way to erase it. And he wasn't sure he even wanted to try. It was his mom's last day. All he had to do was push down on the button and there she was waving her big red umbrella at him from across the street. Then he'd hear her calling to him, "Wait, Martin, you'll get soaked; I'll come get you." He'd reverse this and listen again to her low scratchy voice. He just loved his mom's voice. Then the tape went on. He hated this part. He didn't want to watch his mom step in front of the green car coming down the street. He didn't want to see her shiny red boots come out from between two parked cars. She should have gone to the light at the corner. It was the very thing she always scolded him about. Then he'd watch with horror as his mom flew into the air and came down in slow motion to the street. There was a slight bounce as she hit the rain-blackened street. He started to run pell-mell. He got to her just as the driver of the green car did.

"God, kid," the man moaned. "She stepped right out in front of me. She never even saw me."

Martin reached for his mom's arm and climbed in under it. "Mom, you okay? It's me, Martin."

He heard the sirens. He saw the orange and blue car pull up. Mr. Herst, his teacher, stood over him and lifted him out from his mother's arms. The paramedics moved in. He saw his mom slipped onto a stretcher and disappear through the gaping doors of the ambulance.

"Let me go, Mr. Herst. They're taking my mom. She's hurt. I have to help her."

Herst paid no attention and hung on to Martin. He held him off the ground tucked under one arm.

"It's okay, Martin, it's okay. I'll drive right behind the ambulance. Your mom's going to be fine. Probably just knocked out. Your dad will be at the hospital."

From the funny angle Herst held him, Martin got a lopsided view of all the kids and their parents standing on the school steps. Herst toted him like a store mannequin to his car. Now the rain pelted against Dr. Griffin's windows and Martin watched it. It was the same kind of pelting rain he saw against his mom's windshield. He saw the police-

4

man go to his mom's car, open the door, take the keys out. The windshield wipers stopped flipping back and forth.

At the hospital when he saw his dad's face, he knew that his mom had stopped, too.

His eyes teared up. Dr. Griffin shook his head.

"Been watching your tape?"

Martin lowered his eyes. He didn't want to look Dr. Griffin in the eye.

"Martin, I've told you before. Everything can be erased. Typewriters erase, computers erase, answering machines erase. Can't you try to erase the parts that hurt so?"

Martin twisted his wrist so that he could see the time. The tears blurred the face of his watch.

"Yep, you're right on time. You're very good at hitting the end of the session right on the button. Okay, Martin, scoot along. See you tomorrow. And think about erasing."

Chapter 2

Martin never had to use his twisted wrist trick to see what time it was at school. History was his last class and watching his pet hate, Saucey Sanders, was like watching a clock. At 2:35 Saucey surreptitiously packed up her L. L. Bean backpack. At 2:40 she yawned and showed off her flashing braces. At 3:01 she began her ritual kick, twitching her Nikes up and down, faster and faster until the bell rang. But today Mr. Herst had a guest speaker and class would run late. This meant that he'd probably have to go right to Dr. Griffin's from the lecture. Martin hoped to get to Mount Auburn before it got dark and they locked the gate. It had rained so hard yesterday that the gate had been closed. He hadn't visited his mom's grave since Sunday.

"So let me introduce Mr. Terry Tellison." Mr. Herst brought the class to order.

A tall, skinny man unwound himself from one of the extra classroom seats down front. He had on a tweed jacket over a sweater. He slipped off the jacket and tossed it on his chair. Mr. Tellison was in his early 30s and looked like a Viking with his thick thatch of red hair and a short red-blond beard.

Mel Eaton had been elected to twist the light dimmer and, as the room darkened, Martin watched the first color slide snap on.

"Now, kids, Mr. Herst told you that I'm a marine archeologist. That means that instead of my digs being in the deserts of Egypt or on the hills of Greece, I dig on the bottom of the sea. The slide you see here is a scale model of the famous English sailing ship, the *Sara More*. I know you've all read about the *Sara*. Now do any of you know what makes my work different from say, a salvaging company, like the one that sacked the *Titanic?*"

Saucey hogged the floor.

"Salvagers sell whatever they dig up to anyone. Archeologists put the stuff in museums where it belongs and where everyone can see it."

"You're dead right. Had salvagers found the *Sara,* they would have made a killing and cheated England right out of a whole chunk of her naval history. *And* the Crown couldn't have done one thing about it. Know why?"

Mel knew. Salvage at sea and treasure hunting in water were the current topics in history class. The kids had read about the *Andrea Doria,* the *Mary Rose,* the *Chitoca,* and the *Titanic.*

"Sure. The *Sara More* was more than twelve miles out. Twelve miles is the limit for a country to lay claim to treasure. You were in international waters."

"And you know something? We weren't that much farther out. Now look at the model. Isn't she a beaut? I had such luck. I found the diary of the ship's doctor in a library at Portsmouth. It had been hidden there for years and years—came out of some old admiral's estate. Well, in his diary—the doctor's name was Roger Shaw—he wrote about how the captain of the *Sara More* was worried about having to carry such an enormous amount of cannon, more than any other ship had ever carried. His concern was not the out-going voyage. He was worried about

7

coming home. Then they'd have not only the cannon but the cargo. He was afraid that if the ship hit a storm, it would simply split and sink from its own weight. He confided to Shaw that if a storm came on he was going to head for Point Pittance, not for Portsmouth. Pittance is a very sheltered spot. He did just that. And, if he hadn't had the bad luck to hit a reef, he would have made it. Instead, the *Sara More,* sailors and all, went down.

"What puzzled the Crown and the people was that there never was so much as a sign of the ship. Not a piece. Not a body washed ashore. Of course, they were simply looking in the wrong place. When I read Shaw's diary, I calculated about where the reef was and where the *Sara* would have struck it. In we went and we found her. And, more luck, the only things that had broken off were the mast and the figurehead. *Sara* sank right down she was so heavy, and sat in the silt. This protected her all these years. She was almost as good as new when we got through all the sand and mud cover."

Mr. Tellison clicked on a new slide. It showed an antique helmet.

"Shaw wrote that he used this to anesthetize his patients. He put the helmet on them and banged on their heads with a wooden mallet. His theory was that vibration numbed pain. At one point in his diary he also says that most of the crew was so numb-brained the helmet really wasn't necessary. And here's . . ." Tellison clicked on another slide.

"What are those things?" Saucey queried.

Martin knew that the board games were backgammon. He'd played it with his mom.

"Don't you recognize them? Those are backgammon sets. We found about twenty of them in the crew's quarters. And see that funny instrument? That's a tabor."

Martin watched Mr. Tellison push down the button. Up came another slide. This one showed the ship's figurehead.

Martin's stomach flopped over. There on the screen was his mom lying on the ocean floor. It was the same color as the wet asphalt street she'd bounced back onto. Her hair had streaked across her face. She looked just like this carved figurehead. Martin turned away. What came up on the screen next was even worse.

"Let me introduce you to a few remaining members of the crew."

The kids laughed. The slide showed several skeletons. Martin's stomach cramped and churned. He clutched his desk till his knuckles turned white. The biggest skeleton was wearing his mom's raincoat. Her red scarf was wound around a bony hand. The skeleton's foot wore his mom's red boot. Martin breathed hard. He knew his lunch was on the UP escalator and he'd better get out. He grabbed his backpack and climbed over the kids in his row. He headed for the door just as Mr. Tellison asked for the lights. He heard him say, "Okay. Next time I see you I can show you the *Sara* being pulled out of her grave and . . ." Martin ran down the hall and headed for some air.

Chapter 3

By the time Martin left Dr. Griffin's office, the soft November light was fading. Martin sprinted as fast as he could. He was good at track and he kept his pace as even as he could so he wouldn't get winded. He *had* to get to Mount Auburn today. What with Mr. Tellison's talk and Dr. Griffin's nougats, he wasn't sure he'd make it to the gate before they locked up. It was maddening. You could get out of the cemetery by standing on the tall markers next to the stone wall, grabbing the iron fence, and climbing onto it. But you couldn't get in. No way.

Mount Auburn Cemetery was stuffed smack in the heart of historic Cambridge just down the way from the famous Old Burying Ground. Only a few old and prestigious families had plots there any more. Martin's mother had made it clear to one and all that when she went she wanted to end up at the golden oldie, Mount Auburn.

"My great, great grandpa bought a plot for twelve. Who he thought would take up the space never entered his head. There are still six empties and that's where I'm going," she'd laughed.

Martin turned the corner and sighed with relief. The gates were wide open. Still running, he skidded onto an old gravel path and started cutting through the monuments. He hopped from stone to stone until he landed next to a marker that read:

JENNIFER MORLEY PRENTISS
1958–1989

"Hi, Mom." Martin perched on the edge of the stone marker right next to his mother's grave. "I thought I'd *never* make it. How are you? We had a special lecture at school today. I cut early, but Uncle Phil was into nougats."

Martin chewed an imaginary nougat and did his best imitation of the doctor. "You'll never have to worry about investments, Martin. You won't have anything to invest if you keep these grades up." Then Martin produced an imaginary handkerchief from his pocket and wiped away the imaginary chocolate from the corners of his mouth.

The cemetery was still soaked from yesterday's storm. Martin got up and put his hand on the Morley monument. He outlined his mom's name with his finger. "I know. I know. Uncle Phil is really trying to help. I don't mean to turn him off. I just can't keep my mind on what he's saying."

The very last bit of sunshine touched Martin's shoulder. He was sweating from the run, and the November day had been one of the last Indian summer days Boston would bask in before winter hit. Martin pulled off his backpack and his sweater. He reached down deep into his bag and rummaged around the bottom. He fished out a big starfish and held it in the light.

"I've got a surprise, Mom. Look. It's our big star. The one we found at the Cape. I thought you'd like to watch it." He carefully placed it smack in the center of the stone marker.

11

"Boy, just look at what the rain has done to these other guys." With his fingernails he managed to pull out a splendid collection of mud-coated shells from the ground around the grave. He spit on them and rubbed them on his pants. When they were clean again, he rearranged them all around the starfish.

"And I bought a moonshell for you. Remember? We saw it at the shell store. Consider it a gift even though your birthday isn't until January. I wanted you to have something new to look at. It must get boring being here all by yourself. I sure miss you."

Martin leaned back on the stone across from his mom's. "Mom, I saw a slide today at a lecture that made me so sad. I want to know something. Are you a skeleton now? The skeleton the archeologist man showed us was just nothing but bones. No hair. Nothing. I had to get out. I couldn't see you that way. You're so pretty." Martin stared at his mother's grave. "I don't suppose there's a chance that you'll ever be back?"

The heavy fringe of Martin's blond eyelashes caught the tears. They hung there a second, then fell. "I don't want to be a crybaby; I know how you hate that. But I think of you all the time, Mom, and I can see you plain as day. And you aren't a skeleton. Not the way I see you."

The last of the sun slipped away and twilight hurried on. "I'd better get going, Mom. You know what a fit Mrs. Grant has if I'm really late and she thinks I've been here."

He slipped on his sweater. It was so quiet and peaceful here. His cassette didn't ever play at Mount Auburn.

Chapter 4

Mrs. Grant was not listening to her Spanish lesson. A male voice droned on and on. "Qué día es, Rosa?"

"Es jueves, no viernes," the machine answered.

Charlotte, Mrs. Grant's huge blue and green parrot, answered the machine. "Wheyves, wheyves. *Bare*naise, barenaise."

Mrs. Grant reached over and snapped off the lesson and stood up. She patted her parrot on the beak. "Charlotte, you always make Friday sound like a sauce. It's *bee*-air-nays not *bare*naise." The parrot rubbed her beak up and down Mrs. Grant's finger. Mrs. Grant checked her watch.

"You know, Charlotte, it's six-thirty and our Mr. Martin isn't home yet. I'm going to give him five more minutes to show. Then I'm getting out the car and fetching him. He doesn't kid me. I know where he is. And *you* know how *I* feel about visiting *that* place. Specially in the dark."

Mrs. Grant was a tall black woman with curly graying hair. She had the carriage and personality and looks that would get her a part in any play that called for a beautiful black woman with humor. She slipped off her apron, turned off the lights over the parrot stand, and dimmed the one that lit the great oil painting of Charlotte. She slipped on her heavy red wool cardigan and searched the pockets for the car keys.

"What *do* I *do* with car keys? I swear there is a trapdoor for keys in this house."

Charlotte screamed out her rage at being left in a dim room. "Lights. Lights!"

"Oh, cut it out, you old phony. You just love the stage. I'll be back in five minutes, and I'm telling you that Martin Prentiss and Mrs. Grant are going to have it out tonight. He may not want to communicate but *I* want to communicate." She found the keys in a kitchen table drawer and picked up the dinner bell from the table. Then she cut through the hall to the garage door.

By the time her blue Chevy drew up to the cemetery gates, they were shut tight.

"Never fails!"

She grabbed the dinner bell from the dashboard and got out and slammed the door, leaving the car lights on. She headed for the gate entrance and stuck her hand through the heavy wrought iron fence. Then she rang the bell as hard as she could.

"Oh, boy!" Martin looked startled. "That's Mrs. Grant. She's really going to be mad. I got to run, Mom. See you tomorrow. Sleep tight."

The bell continued to jangle. Martin jumped from one stone to the next. He knew his way around in the dark. He'd have to use Mr. Witherton's marker to grab hold of the fence. He cleared the top and landed right in back of Mrs. Grant. She froze at the sound. She spun around and saw Martin standing there with a very sheepish expression on his face.

"Dear Lord Almighty! You just took ten years off my short life, boy. Now get in that car. THIS MINUTE!"

14

Mrs. Grant backed up the Chevy and did a U-turn. She called it her "Heimlich maneuver." The car disappeared down the dark street.

"Does it *ever* occur to you that when you don't come home, I get worried? I'm responsible for your where-abouts. I'm having a talk with your father tonight—if *he* comes home."

Martin had his cassette on and running. He didn't hear Mrs. Grant. He watched his mom wave and call "Wait Martin, you'll get soaked." There—right on his own screen—was his mom in her red raincoat. She smiled at him. This was his favorite, favorite part. He didn't even realize that they were sitting in the garage. Mrs. Grant had turned the motor off and was staring at him.

Chapter 5

Martin watched Mrs. Grant adjust the blind in the dining room so that the sun no longer glared in his eyes. The dining room was one of the prettiest rooms in the house. A long shiny antique table was surrounded by four red and white upholstered armchairs and four regular dining chairs. Their seats were in the same fabric as the armchairs, and the curtains matched. The rug was a truly fine Oriental that had been in the Morley house since it had been built. That was over a hundred years ago. The table was set for two. Martin sat on a regular chair but one of the comfortable armchairs was pulled up at his father's place. The view from the room through the tall paned French windows looked like a painting. There was a huge oak tree centered in the impeccably groomed yard. By now most of the leaves were hanging by threads and had turned a tawny gold.

"Your father will be down in a minute and I have just one thing to say to you. I'm going to be up-front with you. I'm telling him where you hang out or you can tell him yourself. Take your choice. I am not going to that cemetery one more time. Every time you go there, Martin, you make it harder on yourself—to say nothing about me. Eat your toast.''

Martin gnawed at the corner of his toast and smiled at Mrs. Grant.

''Don't you turn your charm on me. I've had it.'' She swung open the door to the kitchen, held it with her foot, reached around the corner, and swooped up an egg holder, a toast rack, and a thermos of coffee. She placed everything down at the setting opposite Martin. Then she piled up the early special mail deliveries. She put the three newspapers the professor read in a neat stack and picked up her bell. She headed for the bottom of the steps and rang it to a fare-thee-well. Professor Prentiss, carrying his coat and case, arrived on cue. He kissed Martin on the top of his head.

''Hi, son. What cooks, huh?''

Martin gave him a ''not-much'' shrug, knowing his dad would immediately pour his coffee and dig into his mail. His dad handled mail just like Dr. Griffin handled his candy box. The only difference was that his dad didn't punch the bottoms of the letters. He held them up to the light.

The phone rang and Mrs. Grant answered. There was a phone stand at the table right at Professor Prentiss's elbow.

Mrs. Grant put her hand over the mouth of the phone.

''It's Mr. Curtis from State.'' She handed the professor the phone. He bit into his toast. While he chewed he listened carefully. He uh-huh-huh-ed a lot, then took a sip of coffee.

''I can't, Bob. I wish I could but I'm booked solid.''

Martin looked around the room. He could still see his mom sitting at the head of the table. That was *her* place. She'd be reading the financial section of the *New York Times*. It was the one part of the paper his father wanted. She'd read tempting bits of news to her husband. His mom was a real early bird. His dad was not. By the time John

17

Prentiss made it to breakfast, his wife had perused all three papers and was on her third cup of coffee.

Mrs. Grant poured hot coffee. The doorbell rang. The phone rang again. This time the professor picked it up himself. "I just this minute talked to him. He's at his office." He hung up and looked woefully at Mrs. Grant. The doorbell rang again.

Martin's father signaled to Martin to answer the door. Martin was delighted for the reprieve. He did not want to talk to his dad about his report card *or* about Mount Auburn. He softly padded out of the dining room. His dad was on the phone again. He signed for special mail and put the envelope on the hall table where his dad would see it on his way out. Then he hightailed it up the stairs and sat on the top step. It was too early to head for the school bus. If Mrs. Grant wondered where he'd gone, she'd just think he was upstairs getting his gear together.

"Harlan, yes. It's set. It's been negotiations, one after another. Nothing with Mrs. Thatcher is impossible. She's quite a doll. Oh, come on, that's just your Irish getting in the way. Listen, I'll go with you. Yes, I'll grab the five o'clock American."

Mrs. Grant brought more toast and an egg.

"Where's Martin?"

"That's a good question," snapped Mrs. Grant. "I ask myself that every single evening."

"What do you mean?"

"Look, Professor, I told Martin I was going to be up-front with you. And I'm going to be. I think the best thing I can do for all of you, *and for myself,* is quit."

Martin's mouth dropped open. He thought she was going to complain about him. A sick feeling rose in his stomach. Mrs. Grant couldn't quit. If she left, the place would really be a tomb. He worried himself down to a lower stair.

"WHAT ARE YOU SAYING? YOU CANNOT QUIT!" His father was shouting. "WHAT IN GOD'S NAME

WOULD WE DO WITHOUT YOU? You glue this place together."

"To be perfectly candid, Professor, my glue has come unstuck. Martin's not better. I think he's worse. Going farther and farther away from me. I can't get to him. And to top it all he's in that cemetery *every* day after school. He sits there till it's dark and I have to go get him."

"He's supposed to be with Phil Griffin *every* day after school."

"Well, that's why he's so late. He runs right off to the cemetery from Dr. Griffin's office. That's some therapy."

The professor stirred his coffee and stirred and stirred. "Listen, Mrs. Grant, I've got an idea. What if I asked Dorr to come on home for a month or so? She'd be company for Martin."

"Professor, you know I love Dorr. She's a doll. But she's not the answer. But maybe she would help him."

Martin came back into the dining room. Mrs. Grant had gone to the kitchen. "Gotta go, Dad."

"Hey, Mart, what about dinner tonight? Just us. We'll eat junk."

Martin shook his head and smiled. The professor pulled him toward him and gave him a hug.

Mrs. Grant came in to pick up the dishes. She wondered how one did quit a job. She certainly hadn't been successful. She also knew that Martin, in spite of her lecture, would do a rerun to the cemetery and she knew that Professor Prentiss was going to catch the five o'clock American flight to Washington and that Martin would eat with her. She flopped the door open into the kitchen.

She checked her watch, took an address book from a cabinet drawer, picked up a paring knife, and went to the phone. She dialed at least twelve digits and waited for a ring. Martin quietly let himself out the side door.

Chapter 6

Martin snapped on Julia Child. Not that he loved to watch her all that much. He liked to superimpose his mom's head over Julia's and pretend that they were all back in the kitchen downstairs. His mom had loved to cook. Mrs. Grant and his mom would try anything. The more chopping, the better. His mom had called chopping "life therapy." They'd always let him help. He could cut French beans with the best of them, and he could frost the sides of cakes. He would set up the Cuisinart as Mrs. Grant warned him for the zillionth time, "Do not put anything in that machine unless that button is OFF. I do not want to be looking around for a finger."

Suddenly, standing right in front of Julia, was his sister, Dorr. Dorr with her long red hair and blue eyes.

"Boy, are you deaf? I almost knocked my knuckles off trying to get through to you."

She sat on the bed next to him. Martin hadn't seen much of Dorr since she started college, and suddenly he realized how much he had missed her. He always had fun playing around with Dorr, even though she was a lot older. She was plenty quick with the ball.

"It's your wicked stepsister." Dorr fluffed his hair up and tickled him. "Why do I say that? I'm not your wicked stepsister, I'm your wicked half sister. Funny, I get this weird picture of half a person strutting around." She nuzzled her nose into the warm back of his neck. "But which half, heh, heh. Which half?" She curled up on the bed next to him, and they watched Julia together.

Dorr knew that Martin really had no idea of what her role in the Prentiss household had been. For him, she'd been there from day one. Dorr's face still reddened when she remembered all the scuttlebutt around town when her dad left her mom to marry Jennifer Morley. She'd been devastated. People had called her dad a "cradle snatcher," a "student eater." Her mom was outraged.

"Imagine how this looks! It's disgusting. Marrying a student half his age."

Her dad had fought for joint custody and won. Jenny had knocked herself out to make Dorr feel at home. As it turned out, she was happier with Jenny that she was at the little house her mom had bought. She called it "outrage house." Dorr understood Martin's not talking. She had clammed up for a whole year after her parents' divorce. Maybe clamming up ran in the family. Maybe that was what Prentisses do when they're traumatized. She looked at Martin and her heart ached. She knew what it was like to miss someone. She had missed her room, her home, and her own mom and dad in it. She'd hated commuting from house to house. She never felt she belonged anywhere. But little by little, Jenny had taken care of all that, and had started her talking again. And Jenny had shared Martin with her from the first, probably shared him more than she would have if she been his full sister. Jenny insisted that she vacation with them. Jenny made her part of the family, and when Jenny's famous anthropologist sister, Hortense,

21

came on her yearly book tours, they always had fabulous times. Dorr loved Aunt Horty.

"Have you heard a peep out of Aunt Horty, Mart?"

Martin turned over on his side. Dorr put her arm around his shoulder. "Don't worry. I don't care if you don't talk. I was just remembering the summer Aunt Horty came with her chimp. Pop flipped out. It's funny how he and Aunt Horty have never hit it off. Maybe she'll come this spring. She's got a new book coming out."

She checked her watch as Julia signed off with her "bon appétit." "Hey, Mart, give me the channel gismo. Dad's on TV right now on the *Boston Brahmins*. We ought to watch him."

Martin reached under his pillow and pulled it out. Dorr clicked around till she tuned in on the show. It was already in progress. There was Kathie Sparling, the hostess, and there, big as life, was Professor Prentiss.

Martin sat up to watch. When the camera closed in on the other guest, Martin flinched. It was the skeleton man from school. Martin shut his eyes tight. He didn't want to see those slides again.

Dorr watched with fascination as the camera zoomed in on a small-scale version of the *Sara More*. She had no idea that her dad had anything to do with the excavation of that famous boat. She knew he was being talked about for a major post in the government. She'd seen items in the newspaper columns, but she had no idea it involved a boat. What did her dad's position as chair of the political science department at Harvard have to do with this? She concentrated.

"You're really going to be able to pull up the whole boat?"

"You bet we are," said Mr. Tellison. "I want to make a museum out of it. Do a complete restoration of the boat. Make the *Sara* as glamorous as she was. And we want to

22

do it in Portsmouth, where she was originally built and fitted out."

"And you should just see some of the historical gems Terry has already pulled out," Professor Prentiss said proudly. "Cannon, pewter, gold ingots. He actually found a keg of butter with big fingerprints in it. Guess those old tars weren't into butter knives."

"And what does it take to get this all up and on shore? The ship, that is, not the butter?" Sparling asked.

Tellison replied, counting the items off on his fingers, "A giant steel cradle, a lifting frame, a top-notch group of pros, and, of course, plenty of dollars."

"Is that where you come in, Professor Prentiss?"

"Not so much with dollars. I was able to give Terry a different kind of support. Luckily, I was able to call in some favors and tug on some well-placed strings. Terry was able to get security and the support of the British government. And why not? He's giving England back some fantastic treasures."

"Do you feel exhilarated about the whole thing now that it's a *fait accompli?*"

"Actually," Terry laughed, "I feel more like the wreck."

"Your wife must be excited. Has she been with you on the entire project?"

Terry looked uncomfortable, then laughed. "My wife doesn't even like to look at water."

"I'll be happy to take her place on the big day. I understand that *National Geographic* will be there in England the day you pull it up—that's (she checked her clipboard) June twenty-third. Right?"

"That's the big day."

"Well, count me in. We've been chatting with . . . "

Dorr turned down the volume and Martin unscrewed his eyes for the closing shot of the studio and the credits.

"Pop was good." She got up and peered out the window. "As a matter of fact, here he comes now. How come he's here? He was just on TV. Come on. We'll go say hello and congratulate him.''

Dorr headed for the door. "Come on, Martin."

Martin reached over for his sneakers and began to tie one. He heard his dad come in the front door.

"Anyone home? Hello!"

Dorr rounded the stairwell just as he hung up his coat. Mrs. Grant hustled in from the kitchen.

"You're certainly early tonight."

"How come you're here when we just watched you on TV?" Dorr gave him a hug. "You were good."

The professor beamed. "They taped us about an hour ago. Where's Martin? I need some masculine company."

"Chauvinist!" Dorr shook her finger at him. "You don't need any company with all the makeup you have on."

"Oh, oh, I forgot to wipe it off!" He pulled out his pocket handkerchief.

Mrs. Grant made a run for it. "Oh no, you don't! You go in the washroom and use Kleenex."

Prentiss spied Martin on the bottom step and held out his arms. "Come over here! I want a hug."

Martin hugged him and headed for the living room couch. He dug himself deep into the corner.

"Did you see the whole show?" Prentiss called from the washroom.

"Almost. Boy, is that Tellison guy a hunk!" Dorr called back.

"Forget it, hon, he's married." Prentiss came in and headed for the bar.

Mrs. Grant hung around arranging chair pillows and plumping them up. "Oh, Professor, I *knew* I had something to tell you. I spoke with Ms. Hortense. She was headed for the airport."

The professor did a military turn at the bar. "Where's she going?"

24

"She's not going. She's coming!" Mrs. Grant grinned.

Martin felt a wave of warmth in his tummy. Aunt Hortense *was* coming. Had Dorr known? She was just talking about how maybe she'd come. Aunt Horty always made him feel good. He noticed the keen look of displeasure on his dad's face. And Dorr couldn't have known. She looked amazed.

"Coming where?"

"Coming here! She's leaving Nairobi today and she'll be in London tomorrow."

"Oh, God," he moaned. "When does she arrive?"

"Around noon, if the plane's on time. Isn't that great, Martin?"

Martin smiled. He would be glad to see her. He'd always felt like a filling for a sandwich when his mom and Aunt Horty got together. He sat between them at the movies, he sat between them at the table, he walked between them to Harvard. But the last time he'd seen her was at his mom's funeral. He'd sat between Aunt Horty and his father. She held his hand. He couldn't say anything at all to her. He couldn't believe what had happened. He'd heard Aunt Horty begging his dad to let her take him back with her to Africa, but his dad nixed the idea. Martin heard from her regularly but he hadn't answered her letters. She'd call and talk to Mrs. Grant. He couldn't talk. He knew when he saw her that he'd cry. She looked so much like his mom it was scary.

"Well, I don't know about the rest of you, but I'll be glad to see her. She's a real nice distraction." Mrs. Grant stacked logs in the fireplace and left them for the professor to light up.

"Distraction? *Distraction?* Did you say distraction? Hortense Morley is a *disaster,* not a distraction! I certainly hope she's not bringing that ugly beast with her."

"You know, Professor, I was so excited when I talked to her I forgot to ask if Philippa was coming."

25

Professor Prentiss fixed himself a drink. Dorr got a coke for herself and for Martin. "This is certainly not what I need now! Hortense and her damned chimp," the professor complained.

Martin remembered that the only time his mom and dad had ever fought was after the chimp bit his dad on the ear. His mom and aunt giggled and laughed about it. His dad roared with anger. Martin felt a wave of excitement. Aunt Horty would be here in the morning. Maybe she'd go with him to Mount Auburn. She'd understand why he needed to go. Maybe she could make his dad and Mrs. Grant understand. Things had to get better. They couldn't get worse.

Chapter 7

Martin saw Aunt Horty first. He stood by the living room window and saw a cab drive up and his heart flopped. For a second he was sure it was his mom. The cab was crammed with luggage. Aunt Horty wasn't going to stay just a few days. That was for sure. Martin's aunt was taller than his mom but they had the same easygoing, kind of loping swagger. Hortense wore jeans, a plaid shirt, and a huge sweater, and carried a Sherpa coat which she plopped down on the hood of the cab.

"Yoo-hoo, gang. I'm here. Honk your horn, will you?" she called to the driver.

Mrs. Grant came running from the kitchen. Dorr came flying down the front stairs. His dad sauntered out from the library. Martin simply stood and watched the hullaba-loo from the window.

He saw his dad give Hortense a cool peck on the cheek. He watched the cabbie start unloading the trunk. He watched Mrs. Grant and Hortense hug. Dorr hung onto Hortense's sleeve trying to wedge in her welcome hug and kiss.

"MAAAAAAAARTIN!" His dad's voice commanded

his appearance. Martin walked to the front door and down the steps. He tried to smile but his throat hurt. It ached when he looked into Aunt Horty's eyes. He didn't want to cry. Anything but that, not in front of his dad. Aunt Horty swept him right off his feet and swung him around and kissed him over and over. "I'm sooooo glad to see you. I could eat you with a spoon." Martin hung on to her, afraid that if he let go he would just wail. And he was determined not to cry—no way.

Professor Prentiss cleared his throat. "Ah, Hortense, your bearer is trying to get a signal through to you."

Hortense still hung on to Martin. The professor pointed to the cabbie. Hortense turned to the driver as if she'd never seen him before. "Oh, who?"

"The driver, Hortense. I think he wants some direction about all this stuff, *and* he probably wants to be paid."

"Of course." She let Martin down, but still hung on to his hand. She peered into the front seat. "Uh-huh."

Then she gave everyone a big smile. "John, dear, do you have some bucks on you? I'm out of tip money. In fact, I'm out of money until I get to the bank."

Once before, after his aunt had visited, Martin remembered his dad complaining. "You know I had to tip every single one of those damned porters. She had sixteen pieces of luggage! How come your sister travels without a dime on her? She acts like she's the Queen!"

Martin's dad went through his billfold. "How much is it?"

"I haven't a clue, darling. Look at the meter."

Mrs. Grant was organizing the bags into four groups and pulling a few pieces up the steps. Hortense and the cabbie were having a conference about the front seat cartons which completely obscured the window and the meter. Martin saw his dad poke his head into the back seat, trying to read the meter. He pulled his head out as fast as he could. A huge sheepdog reared up from the seat and

28

barked and bayed at this intrusion. The cabbie pulled the boxes out and there, sitting bolt upright in the middle of the front seat, was the biggest dog Martin had ever seen.

"Dear God," his dad said to the cabbie. "What is that thing you've got there?"

"Don't ask me." The driver shrugged his shoulders. "Ask her!" He held out his hand and pocketed Prentiss's money. Then he pulled the animal out of his front seat by the leash. Mrs. Grant stared wide-eyed. Dorr ran over to pat the dog's head. Hortense grinned wickedly. His dad's mouth opened. He looked appalled. Martin could remember only one dog bigger than this one, and it had been stuffed.

"*That*," the professor pointed to the dog who had just tripped majestically on the curb, "is *yours?*" The cab drove off.

"No, darling, that is *yours!* It's a present for Martin. Mart, come get your present!" She picked up the dog's leash and held it.

Martin cautiously picked his way through the bags toward the animal. The dog saw him coming and jumped up, putting both his paws on Martin's shoulders, which made them eye-level. Martin looked at this great, hairy beast with awe. Mrs. Grant clapped her hands. "Lord, Martin, that pooch is the same size you are."

"His name is Clovis," said Hortense, handing Martin the leash.

"What a neat name," Dorr said. "Clovis was a Frankish king, Mart, in the fifth century."

Clovis eyed Martin. Martin gently took the dog's paws off his shoulders and patted him. This did it. Clovis jumped up and down with delight. Martin held his leash as best he could, but he was no match for this bundle of fur, certainly not when Clovis decided to head for his dad.

Professor Prentiss sidestepped Clovis's dash for him.

29

"Keep that slobbering mess away from me. I've got my suede pants on."

Martin knew that if push came to shove, Clovis would win over him, hands down. He could hardly hang on at all.

Martin was grateful for Dorr's nattering on.

"You know, he's what's known as a bobtail. Way back in the days of kings, if a man bobbed his dog's tail it meant that the dog was a working dog, and there was no tax levied on him."

Clovis moved to get to the professor. "I'll bob this thing's head off if he doesn't stay away from me. Get down, dog. Martin, I mean it, get that thing away from me. Take him for a walk."

Mrs. Grant tried to help Martin. "Can you manage, honey?"

Martin clung to the leash. He was darned if he was going to let go.

Hortense stepped in between Clovis and Mrs. Grant. "Of course he can manage." Martin felt himself being steered toward the curb. "There, honey, just hold him tight. He probably needs a walk anyway, and he most certainly needs to get away from your father's warm welcome. Let me get my stuff in the house, and then we'll both go for a walk. I'll show you how to keep him in tow."

"Here, Professor." Mrs. Grant pointed out the heaviest pieces of luggage for him to tote. "You take these. Dorr, take these and the tennis racket. I can manage these."

Martin heard his father say in a loud voice, "I see your Aunt Hortense is traveling light."

But nobody could get at Aunt Horty. Nobody.

"Oh, this is just my hand luggage. My bearers will be here later in the week with the big stuff."

Martin pulled at Clovis for all he was worth. "Come

30

on, boy." He whispered, "They don't want you jumpin' on them. You're big."

Clovis did not want to take a walk. Clovis jumped, leaped, wrapped his leash around Martin so that Martin had to unwind himself just to take a step. And in the unwinding he unwound Clovis completely from the choke chain, which hadn't been put on right anyway.

Zip went the dog, up the steps. He was heading for a touchdown on Martin's dad. "Oh, oh," Martin muttered.

The professor, taking the last step and balancing the bags, never saw Clovis attack him from the rear. He did a peculiar two-step to the side, tried to regain his balance, but dropped the bags and fell over one onto the lawn. And once he was down, Clovis was upon him, slathering his face with kisses. It was out-and-out love.

Martin raced up the lawn and tried with all his might to pull Clovis off his dad.

"Come on, Clovis, get off my dad! He doesn't like dogs. Stop kissing him. Stop. Come!" But Martin couldn't budge him. Clovis sat on his dad's knees, pinned down his shoulders with his front paws, and took full advantage of his vulnerability.

"Will you get this mutt off me? Dorr, Hortense, Mrs. Grant. HELP!"

Mrs. Grant stood motionless. Dorr moved to help. Hortense laughed. "My God, will you look at that! John Prentiss playing with that animal. And," she imitated the professor, "you've got your suede pants on!"

Hortense, still laughing, grabbed the chain and slipped it over the dog's neck correctly. Then she gave a good jerk, and Clovis reluctantly had to get off his new love. Dorr couldn't keep a straight face as her father tried to get up. His face was wet with slobbery kisses. Mrs. Grant was wiping tears from her face. And then they all heard it. Martin started to chuckle. He was holding his sides. It was such a beautiful sound even his father, wiping his face, had to smile.

"You've got to learn that no one can sit on my dad." Martin was able now to pull the dog to his side. "Aunt Horty, this is one big animal you brought me."

The professor finally got to his feet. He patted Martin on the back. "Thanks, Mart, for rescuing me. Now go take your walk and try to stay on *your* feet."

Martin knew very well who was going to take whom for a walk. For the first time in months Martin felt lighter. Some of the heavy weight he'd been toting in his body was gone. "Come on, boy, let's run."

The whole group watched Martin run down the street, a bundle of energetic grey and white hair prancing at his side. Mrs. Grant couldn't keep back the tears. Dorr wiped her eyes. Hortense put her typewriter on her head and pointed to the door. Prentiss opened it for her and she walked in, smiling, balancing the machine beautifully. The professor couldn't help but laugh.

Chapter 8

Martin, Dorr, and Mrs. Grant were all in the kitchen. Martin had set up a big water bowl on the floor of the extra pantry. Mrs. Grant handed him a big plastic place mat. "Here, this will catch some of his slobbering."

Martin pulled Clovis in to see where the water was. "Here, boy, here's your drinking fountain." Clovis promptly put his paw in it.

"No, no, Clovis. It's for a drink, not a dunk." Martin went for a refill. Mrs. Grant mopped up the floor. Clovis got the point the second time, and gratefully lapped up the water.

"Would you believe him?" Martin said to Dorr and Mrs. Grant. They answered together, *"No!"*

Mrs. Grant was making a potpie crust. Dorr was shelling peas. Mrs. Grant shoved the carrots at Dorr, pushed the peas over to Martin. "Here, Martin, you can do the peas."

Clovis flopped down next to Martin's feet, exhausted. The kitchen crew worked along happily and silently. Clovis snored. They heard Aunt Horty come down the stairs.

Martin and Dorr were going to join her, but then they heard her talking to the professor in the den. The den was right next to the kitchen and they could hear everything that was said.

Aunt Horty made a yawning sound. "Hmmmm, good to be home. I'm so glad the puppy liked you, John. It's important that a pup likes the people around him."

Mrs. Grant looked at Dorr and Martin and grinned. They were all ears for the professor's reaction.

"You keep using the word 'pup.' That is *not* a puppy. That is a horse."

"Why, he's just a few months old. He's still growing. And he's housebroken. That should cheer you up."

"What I'd like to know is who is going to keep that beast in chow?"

"Maybe he can get a job."

Dorr giggled.

"Honestly, Hortense. Do you know what it will cost to feed that mutt?"

"Of course I don't. We kill lions and tigers for our meals. Quit fretting. I'll take him out to dinner whenever I can."

"Why didn't you buy a pussy cat? Cats don't have to be walked, and they take care of themselves, and they don't slobber. I hate animals that slobber."

"Face it, John, you hate animals—period. I'll never forgive you for socking Philippa."

Dorr smiled at Martin to share the Philippa experience with him.

"Your ape bit me."

"That's because you scared her. And she's not an ape. She's a chimp."

"Whatever she is she was banging on my typewriter."

"She was not banging. She was typing."

"Monkeys don't type."

"Mine does. When you hit her you set her work back

34

six months. Would you like it if I flung a book at one of your gifted students?''

''My gifted students don't climb walls or sink their teeth into you. It cost me seventy bucks to get shots.''

''Don't forget that Philippa had to have shots, too. I was petrified that she'd catch your distemper.''

The three kitchen helpers all laughed. Mrs. Grant put her finger to her lips and whispered. ''Quiet. If we're going to eavesdrop, we have to be quiet.''

Martin leaned over and petted the big dog. Under his breath he said, ''Better watch it, pal. Dad doesn't like to be bit.'' He shook up the dog's ruff. All ninety pounds of animal groaned with pleasure. ''Isn't he wonderful? Wouldn't mom have just loved him?''

''She sure would.'' Mrs. Grant gave Martin a big grin and took the bowl of peas he had shelled. She was amazed Martin was not only talking but had actually mentioned his mom.

Mrs. Grant added the carrots and peas to some water and began to bring them to a boil for her sauce. They all tuned in again on the conversation from the den.

''How long are you going to perch here?''

''I'm not perching. Don't forget that half this house is mine.''

''Well do I know it. I wish I had the bucks to buy you out.''

Martin looked at Dorr. It was a worried look.

''My half is not for sale.''

''What made you suddenly decide to visit now? Did Dorr write to you?''

Dorr looked worriedly at Mrs. Grant.

''No, AT&T is responsible.''

''Dorr called?''

''No, Mrs. Grant did.''

''*She* phoned Africa?''

''Collect.''

35

Mrs. Grant rolled her eyes skyward and banged her bosom with her hand.

"That was totally out of line."

"She's smart, that's what. Worth her weight in gold."

"How would you know? I pay her now."

"Honestly, John, is money all you ever think about?"

"When it comes to this falling down wreck of a house, yes."

"I pay my half of the taxes."

"Yes, but who do you think keeps this four floor white elephant landmark glued together? Do you have a clue what it costs in this day and age to paint this heap? This house drinks Dutch Boy for cocktails. You New England rich are all alike. Frrrrruuuuuuugggalllll. That's how you stay rich."

"OK. OK. I get the point."

Martin hated it when his dad and Aunt Horty talked about money. He decided to head for his room until Mrs. Grant rang her dinner bell. Dorr decided to do some reading in her room. They went up the stairs together. Clovis climbed after them, missing several steps on the way. "He is some bumbler." Martin laughed.

Dorr headed up the next flight. Martin and Clovis headed for his bed. Martin patted the bed and Clovis managed, after a few tries, to get up on it. Then the dog stretched out as if the bed had been made for him and him alone. Martin pushed him over. "Come on fellow. Give me a break. You can't have the whole bed." Martin tucked his arms behind his head and sighed. It had been some day. It was wonderful having Aunt Horty here. He realized he hadn't even given his cassette a thought since she had arrived. He didn't want to lose sight of his mom. "You should have known my mom, Clovis. You would have loved her."

36

Chapter 9

Martin chewed his cereal and watched his dad dial a number. Aunt Horty was working the *New York Times* crossword in ink. This enraged his dad. He did them in pencil. He had suggested that Hortense might like to subscribe to her own copy of the paper; that way they'd each have a puzzle. Aunt Horty thought this was a terrible idea. "What a waste! Two copies of this giant gazette. There's enough here for a family of twelve to read."

"Terry, how are you? I think it's great. You'll be so rich and famous you won't know what to do. Why are you sneezing? Have you got a cold?" His dad waited for an answer. "You're allergic to a cat? Why do you keep it? You're telling me that *you* bought it? For your wife? You must be mad. Get her a hamster. Or better yet," his dad grinned and watched for a reaction from Aunt Horty, "we have a big slobbering dog here that you could have."

He got his reaction. Aunt Horty put down the puzzle and glared at him. Martin frowned at him. "Oh, well, next week. Maybe Thursday. Take something for your allergy."

He hung up, tied the sash of his robe tighter, and stood up. He took his coffee with him. "Well, my dears, I am going to shower." They heard him pad up the steps.

All was quiet. Aunt Horty worked on her puzzle. Martin sloshed his milk from side to side. Then they heard the yell from upstairs.

"Martin, get up here and get your soggy dog out of my shower!"

"Oh, oh," Martin moaned. "I must have left Dad's bathroom door open. Clovis loves his shower. What'll I do?" Aunt Horty grabbed Martin and they headed for the kitchen. Mrs. Grant got the signal and raced for a roll of paper towels. Then she grabbed two bath towels out of the hamper.

"Here, get up there fast and bring the dog down. Wrap him in these so he won't drip all the way back."

Martin raced up. His dad just pointed at the shower. Martin reached in and grabbed Clovis by his chain and pulled. Out came a soaking wet sheepdog. His dad must have had the water running on him for at least five minutes. He wrapped the big towels around Clovis and pulled him out of the bathroom.

"Come on boy. *Come on!*" Clovis trotted along looking like some strange little camel.

"Keep that animal out of here! Do you hear me?"

Martin tried to pull Clovis down the stairs. It wasn't easy. By the time he got him to the kitchen Martin was almost as wet as Clovis.

"Clovis was asleep in Dad's shower. Dad just never looked and turned on the water. You'd have thought being pelted by water would have wakened him up," Martin said dispiritedly. He took some other dirty towels from Mrs. Grant and tried to make a dent in the drying process.

"I'll be at this all day!" he said disgustedly.

38

"No, you won't." Aunt Hortense sat down for another cup of hot coffee. "Go upstairs and put some dry clothes on and bring me my hair dryer. The big one. We'll have a styling session down here."

Martin felt better in dry jeans. He went to Aunt Horty's bathroom, found the dryer, and ran down the steps to the kitchen. Aunt Horty got up, sat on the floor, plugged the dryer in and pulled Clovis down by her on the floor.

"Here, Mart, help me." Mrs. Grant took the soaking wet towels and headed for the basement washer and dryer.

Clovis was like a nervous lady on her first visit to a beauty salon. He shook and twirled and turned, trying to avoid the hot air. Finally Hortense got the dog back to a fluffy beast. Actually, Martin thought Clovis looked better than ever.

Aunt Horty looked out the window as she wrapped the cord around her dryer. "Martin, let's go for a walk. Let's go to the beach. It's too pretty a day to stay in."

"Can we take Clovis, or will he get all wet again?"

"Can we take Clovis? Where have we been that we haven't had Clovis?"

Mrs. Grant was unstacking the dishwasher. "You want some sandwiches for a picnic?"

"Oh, yes!" Martin said excitedly. "And some chocolate chip cookies for Clovis." Mrs. Grant took some bread and deviled ham out of the refrigerator. "Deviled ham okay?"

"Yes," Aunt Horty said, "perfect. Do we have any watercress?"

Martin went to get the cookies.

Mrs. Grant took a handful out of the box and wrapped them in plastic wrap. Clovis went mad insisting he have one right now. Mrs. Grant indulged him with two cookies.

"Do you know the other day when I was at the checkout counter at the supermarket, the checker said, 'Your family

39

sure do like chocolate chip cookies.' I said, 'They're not for the family, they're for our dog.' Well, you should have seen her face.''

Mrs. Grant watched the three of them head for the car. She leaned on the banister of the front porch. She took a deep breath and waved when they tooted the horn and sped off. It had been a wonderful weekend.

Chapter 10

Even though it was almost December, Boston was having its last fling with a warm sun. It was one of those fluky days when huge clouds flew like blimps over the city. All they needed was "Fuji Film" written on them.

Clovis occupied the entire back seat of the car and sat up straight. His hair blew every which way.

"You know, Aunt Horty," Martin said, turning around to watch Clovis, "if you were driving behind us, you'd think a wild-haired old lady was at the wheel."

"Don't kid yourself, a wild-haired old lady *is* driving."

They approached Woods Hole and a beach. They had no trouble finding a parking spot. The place was empty. They unloaded their shopping bag and blanket, left the top down, and carefully locked the car.

As they neared the dunes the sun seemed to turn off for Martin and the wind got cold. The last time he'd been on this beach he'd been with his mom. He could see her clear as day. She'd kicked off her shoes, scrunched her tanned toes in the sand, and high tailed it to the water's edge.

He saw her cup her hands to her mouth and shout at

him. "Come on down, scaredy cat, get your shoes off. The water is beautiful." He had taken off his shoes and skipped down the dune right into her arms. They'd walked hand in hand along the shore picking shells.

"Oh, Martin, isn't this great. Being here. Being here with you." She'd looked at him like she looked at paintings in the museum. "You know, you are my favorite child."

Martin remembered laughing and saying, "I'm your *only* child. Of course I'm your favorite."

"I might have ten more if I thought they'd all come out like you. Then you'd have to fight for your rights."

He'd looked her right in the eye. "No, I wouldn't. I'd still be your Number One favorite."

"I suppose you would be!" She'd hugged him and they'd walked again.

This was the first memory that Martin had of his mom that hadn't been taped on that terrible day. He could enjoy this tape.

He looked up and saw Aunt Horty watching him.

"Want to try another beach?"

"Nope, let's go on."

Clovis tangoed his way through the lapping surf.

"Don't let him get all wet, Martin. He's going to smell like an old army blanket. Besides he's already had his bath for today."

Martin called Clovis and the dog hurried up the dune, sliding backwards at each step. "That dog is terrific, Aunt Horty, I just love him."

"Come on," Aunt Horty said, picking up the small lunch case and undoing Clovis's chain to let him run. "Let's find a place to pitch our tent."

They walked along together. Martin spotted a pretty shell and pocketed it.

"I thought you weren't visiting Mount Auburn."

"I try not to go every day, but it's hard."

"I know, Mart, but you're spooking everyone out. No one can figure out why anyone would want to hang out in a cemetery. *Especially* Mrs. Grant."

"I know," Martin said sadly. He got up and headed to the edge of the water. He knew Aunt Horty was coming up right behind him. He hoped she wouldn't bring up the cemetery again. But she did.

"Look, Martin. If you need to go to the cemetery to get over your sads, I don't see anything wrong with it."

Martin felt the gloom sit right down on him. The cassette began to play. He saw the man in the green car. He saw the hospital waiting room. He still couldn't believe that his mom was really dead. How could it have happened so fast? She was there one minute and then gone. Gone forever. It had only been last summer that he and his mom had been to this very beach. Six months. She'd been gone six whole months.

Aunt Horty gave him a tap and said, "Come on. I thought we were going to walk."

She took long strides and Martin had to keep up a good pace even to stay behind her. "Martin, you know people have a lot of trouble when they want so desperately to help you and you won't let them. They get discouraged."

Martin figured Aunt Horty was talking about Dr. Griffin. He did seem sad. But Martin didn't feel he could talk about that day to Dr. Griffin. No way.

"It's like you've gone to another planet. First we lose Jenny and then you." She made like she was dialing a phone. "Hello, Earth to Saturn. It gets harder and harder to get to you, and you have a harder and harder time trying to get back to earth. We need you here, honey. You have to start working at school and get back into life."

Martin pitched stones into the water. Aunt Horty stopped to watch. She put the case down on the sand and watched him try to make the stones skim.

"Here, Mart, watch me." She reached down and picked

up a handful of flat stones. "You have to hold it like this." She opened her palm for Martin to see. "Now, throw it like this." Aunt Horty did a pitcher's windup and her stone did three skips.

"So, back to school. Do you think now that I'm here you can get back in the swing?"

Martin shrugged.

"Honey, you have to. None of us knows what to do. Can *I* do anything?"

Martin didn't know if he could explain how he felt; how much he blamed himself for his mom's not being here.

"Nothing is the same anymore, Aunt Horty." He tried to keep from crying. Then Aunt Horty sat down and dragged him into her arms. "I know, it's rotten. Just rotten luck."

Martin felt her arms close around him. They sat that way for a minute, not talking. He felt her warmth. He smelled her special perfume. It was almost like having his mom back. He tried to keep his voice from cracking.

"See, Aunt Horty, Dr. Griffin doesn't understand why my cassette is important. It's all I've got left of mom. It keeps her alive. When I play it, I don't hear anything else. I feel that she's with me. You understand?"

"I do, Martin. But eventually this horror trip will fade. You'll remember all the good things and you'll put aside that awful day. I promise you."

"It's hard, Aunt Horty. If Mom hadn't picked me up, she'd still be alive and here. *I caused* her accident." He couldn't help crying.

Aunt Horty sat up straight. Clovis had joined them and sat next to her. She pushed Martin away and brushed the tears from his cheeks with her scarf.

"Martin, you mustn't feel guilty."

"I can't help it. If Mom hadn't tried to keep me from getting wet—just getting wet, like who cares—she would never have been hit."

"That's just plain silly, Mart. The whole thing is no more your fault than mine. *It was an accident.*"

"No, it was me who caused it. She got hit because of me." He sobbed.

"Martin, listen to me! You cannot carry that guilt. That was a pure accident. It could have happened on any street at any time. There could have been a crack-up."

"No, no, it was me."

"No, no, *it was not.* How do you account for a hundred people from all over the world who get on a plane and it goes down. Why those hundred?"

"But if I'd been the pilot, and Mom was on the plane, I'd have gone with her. I wish I'd been hit instead of Mom."

"Martin, that's absolutely senseless. I am telling you—accidents happen. Neither you nor I can do anything about them. They happen when you least expect them. Jenny was just in the wrong place at the wrong time. She never looked where she was going, and that's how accidents happen. It was not your fault. I'm so, so sad that you had to see it, but it wasn't anything you could do anything about—or you would have done it."

Martin let the tears fall. Aunt Horty kept mopping them up.

"Martin, do you believe me? Do you have faith in me?"

Martin nodded. He did believe Aunt Horty and he trusted her.

"Your mom's accident was a fluke. It was just her time. While she was here, she had a wonderful life. She loved living. She loved your dad. She loved you. I don't know anyone who got a bigger kick out of life. Now she's gone. Much too early, but there's nothing we can do about it. She wasn't sick. We didn't have to watch her linger on and on. She just went." Aunt Horty snapped her fingers. "She certainly would hate to think you were mourning her

45

like this. Climbing into a shell and not talking. You know how she'd hate that. She'd want you to get on with your life. She'd want you to be a good football player. She'd want you to get good grades. Make her proud. Understand? You have to do that for her. Can you?''

Martin nodded again. He wasn't sure about the good grades, but he used to play pretty good football on the junior team.

Aunt Horty stood up and pulled him up. She put her arm around his shoulder. ''Come on, let's get out of here. The wind is getting to me.''

They found a little cove out of the breeze. They didn't even open the sandwich case. Martin was thankful. He didn't think he could keep a sandwich down.

By three o'clock, the satin smooth finish of the ocean had been blown into sharp pleats. Martin found more shells.

''Come on, Martin, I'm getting cold. Let's go and get on with our lives. What do you think?'' Aunt Horty gave him one of her great smiles. He smiled back.

They folded the blanket, picked up the case. Martin put Clovis's chain back on and they all headed up to the car. Hortense put the top up and Martin was glad of the warmth of the car.

As Aunt Horty started the car, she glanced at Martin. ''You know I have a swell idea. Let's stop by Mount Auburn and you can leave your shells and I can say hello to Jenny.''

Martin couldn't believe his ears. He was actually going to be able to visit his mom without worrying about what everyone would say. He gave Aunt Horty a grateful smile and started sorting out the shells he'd collected so he'd have them all ready.

Chapter 11

Martin opened the oven door and peered in. A roast beef sizzled in the pan.

He looked quizzically at Mrs. Grant. "We're having a Sunday dinner on Wednesday?"

"Your pa ordered up a celebration."

"Do you think he's got a permotion of some kind?"

"Could be. And it's *pro*motion."

As Martin walked into the living room, he saw it as it used to be—for the first time in almost a year. Hortense was curled up near the fire working the acrostic and chatting with Dorr. Dorr was munching carrot curls. Clovis was stretched out in front of the fire. Martin looked out the front windows and saw snow whirling on the porch. It felt good. Dorr had just said his dad was probably getting a chair.

"What would dad want with a chair? We have plenty of chairs."

"Not this kind of chair," Dorr patted her armchair. "An academic chair. It's a big honor to get one."

Clovis was up on his feet, hurrying to the front door.

"Hey, that must be Dad," Martin said, trying to head Clovis off at the pass. He missed.

The front door closed and the doors to the living room opened very quickly. Martin didn't even see his dad. He just watched poor Clovis flying through the opened doors and slamming straight into the hall wall. Then his dad slipped quickly around the door and bowed as he came in. Clovis, shaking his head, trotted behind him into the room.

"Wow, that was a mean trick, Dad."

"Martin, it's only a game that your dog and I play. It's called avoiding impact and the rules are his, not mine."

"It must be a real challenge to outwit a Clovis mind," Hortense laughed.

The professor smiled his satisfied smile and rubbed his hands. "How is everyone this snowy evening and what would everyone like to drink?"

"I'll have a Coke, Dad," said Martin. He was still annoyed with his father's treatment of Clovis.

Dorr opted for a Perrier.

"And I will have . . ." Hortense tried to place her order but the professor put up his hand. "I make civilized cocktails. If you want that rot gut and a box of table salt down your gullet, you will have to mix it."

Prentiss made his own drink with care, doled out the other drinks, and stepped aside for Hortense. She lifted a bottle of tequila and filled a shot glass. Then she took a wedge of lime from the saucer, poured a tiny dune of salt on the back of her hand, and headed back to her couch. She picked up the lime wedge and sucked it, then she drank the tequila down in one swig and lapped up the salt.

"Disgusting."

"Wonderful!"

Martin thought it looked like a more interesting drink than his dad's. "So what's up, Dad?" he asked. "Why the roast beef?"

Clovis had quietly sidled up to his dad and had inched

his rump onto the same cushion. The dog put his front paws on the floor. He sat there just as the family sat. No one could say that Clovis didn't participate in the life of the family in a most civilized way. His dad stared at Clovis with a look of amazement.

"Can you believe this?" He pointed at the dog. Clovis was already beginning to drool. "Next he'll want a Mai Tai. Don't you dare drool on me!"

Martin quickly slipped in between his father and Clovis to ward off any dripping. Clovis, Martin, and the professor were now all crammed onto one cushion.

Hortense stared at the threesome. "Aren't you afraid that the couch might tip?"

Martin's dad quickly stood up and walked to the fireplace propping his elbow on the ledge of the mantel. He looked like a very British country gentleman.

"Okay, here's my news—the reason, Martin, for the celebration dinner. How would you all like to toast the new Ambassador to the Court of St. James?"

There was silence, then a shout of joy from Dorr. She ran to him, hugged him, and gave him a big, fat kiss. "That is utterly fantastic, Dad!"

The professor beamed. Hortense walked across and gave him a peck on the cheek. "How did you ever pull that off?"

"I did it the hard way. I earned it."

Dorr went to the kitchen with the news. In seconds, Mrs. Grant bustled out with a bottle of champagne. She shook the professor's hand. "That's real good news."

Martin looked disappointed. "I thought you were getting a chair."

His dad looked puzzled. "A chair?"

Aunt Horty came to the rescue. "Dorr and I were speculating about the celebration dinner. Dorr said she thought you might be getting a chair."

Martin's dad was struggling with the bottle of cham-

49

pagne. Hortense took it from him. "Here, John, just tilt it like this. Hold the cork tight and turn the bottle, not the cork." The cork popped right out and she didn't lose a drop of the golden bubbly.

"Did you learn that in the jungle?"

"Yes. Philippa typed out the directions in case I met anyone civilized here."

Mrs. Grant poured champagne for everyone including herself. The group shouted "To the new ambassador." They all sipped. One sip was enough for Martin. He went and got himself another Coke.

"Will we live in a castle?" he asked his father.

His dad laughed. "Well, hardly a castle. We'll live at Winfield House."

Dorr added, "Winfield House has forty rooms, Mart. It was a gift to the United States from Barbara Hutton, the dimestore heiress."

The professor looked at her lovingly. "Where do you store all that data? Your computer must be on overload most of the time."

"Oh, I don't know, Dad. I just remember what I read."

"Hear that, boy?" Martin patted Clovis's head. "You'll get to sleep in a different room every night. You'll never have to bunk in with dad again." He smiled mischievously.

Everyone avoided looking at him. Martin felt uncomfortable.

"Isn't that right, Dad?"

Hortense went over and sat next to Martin. "Honey, I guess you ought to know right from the start that I wasn't able to take Philippa into England. No way. They have very tough quarantine laws."

"You have to leave an animal in a government kennel for six months," his dad said.

Martin couldn't believe it. "Clovis would have to sit in jail for six months?"

"Right!"

"But, Dad, don't you have some privileges with your job?"

"No, Mart. I wouldn't have that kind of privilege. No one does."

"But Aunt Horty, you brought Philippa right here with you in a taxi."

"That was different. It was the U.S. I brought Philippa in on a promotion–research permit. You can usually get a pet into our country. You just can't take one into England. They worry about their cattle getting hoof and mouth disease."

"But Clovis is healthy. He doesn't have hoof and mouth disease."

"Forget it, Martin," Aunt Horty said sympathetically. "Clovis can stay here with Mrs. Grant and me. You and Dorr will get to go to England. I have to try to do some publicity on my book."

Martin's brain had not absorbed all the facts. He stuttered, "You mean Aunt Horty isn't coming? And Mrs. Grant isn't coming? And Clovis *can't* come!" He felt like someone had socked him in the belly. It was like a rerun of losing Mom. Now he'd lost Aunt Horty *and* Mrs. Grant *and* Clovis.

Instead of answering Martin, John Prentiss stared at Horty. "You mean you'll be staying here? And bringing that ape over? I thought you were heading home."

"This *is* home, John. Since I'm here I can do some work."

The professor looked embarrassed. "Sorry, of course it is."

"Well, I know what I'm going to do." Martin stood up. His voice was steady. "I'm staying here with Aunt Horty and Mrs. Grant and Charlotte and Clovis, and I'm going to my own school. I want to be near Mom."

"You are coming with me!" Prentiss was getting mad. "Do you hear? I cannot believe this whole conversation. I get the best job in the world and we sit here talking about bringing an ape in for a promotion tour and whether a dog can get into England. Listen to me, Martin Prentiss. You and Dorr are coming with me, and THAT'S THAT!'' He pointed at Clovis: "That stays here."

Martin turned to his father. His face was red. "Dorr and you can do whatever you want to do. *Just count me out.*"

Mrs. Grant stood in the doorway with her dinner bell ready to signal dinner. She cased the room and her smile faded.

Martin, in tears, ran by her and up the front stairs. Clovis was right at his heels.

Chapter 12

Charles Street, where lots of Boston's posh antique stores live cheek by jowl, was completely shuttered. The street was dead. "You know, it used to be that everyone went antiquing on Sunday afternoons. Now the really fine shops shut down," Aunt Horty remarked.

Martin walked along silently next to her. "Aunt Horty, isn't there any way you can get Dad to let me stay here? I don't want to go to England. I'll be so lonely again."

Hortense put her arm around his shoulder. "I've done everything I can think of short of bribery. Your pa is stubborn."

"I hate him."

Hortense stopped cold and turned to him. "Martin, don't say that."

"I can't help it. I feel that way. What do I need forty old rooms for? Can't he see that I'm happy here?"

"Honey, you know that your pop and I don't always see eye to eye on stuff. But I do understand him on this one. He doesn't want to lose you. He doesn't want you out of his life. Besides, he'd be the lonely one, and being an Ambassador does call for some family.''

''I could go over for a weekend now and then.''

''He wants you to live with him.''

''But I'd rather live with you, Aunt Horty. I don't think Dad cares about anything but his job. You know he's never once visited Mom. Never even put a flower on her grave.''

''Look, honey, your dad is as lonely for Jenny as you are and I am. But everyone does things differently. You curl up inside. Your dad flings himself into his work outside. You're both running away, but in different directions.''

''I could run away.''

''Where to?''

''I could hide out with Mrs. Grant's nephew. At his house.''

''Where would the cops go first?''

''To Mrs. Grant's nephew's house. I got an idea. Why don't we take the car and head west?''

''How many years do you think I'd get?''

''A lot, probably.''

''Come on, honey, let's get the car and head home. You know what we can do? We can stop at Mount Auburn for a sec if you feel like it. Give you a chance to say a quick goodbye. It won't be forever, Mart. You'll be home on vacation and I'll come to see you, I promise.''

They reached the Morley marker. Martin saw that his shells were covered with snow. He dusted them off with his gloves.

Aunt Horty kept trying to convince him he'd like England. Martin knew he wouldn't.

''It will be a totally new experience. A new country.''

Martin shook his head.

''You know, if I had my druthers, I'd grab you right out from under your dad's nose. But if I were your dad, I wouldn't let you out of my life either.'' She held his face in her hands. "I'm going to miss you.''

"I miss you already. It seems I lose everyone I love.''

Hortense took out a wad of kleenex and dabbed her eyes. They headed back to the street. Suddenly they both turned and blew a farewell kiss to Jenny Prentiss. It seemed to be on cue. Big tears splashed down Aunt Horty's cheeks. Martin held her hand to his cheek and patted it. He knew what it was like to be sad.

Chapter 13

Martin kept his shade up and watched the clouds. The huge plane droned on and on. He couldn't sleep and he wasn't hungry. He knew Dorr was worried. She kept checking on him. His dad, thank heaven, had gone to sleep. He wondered where Clovis was. He looked at his new watch. His dad had given it to him. It had two dials. One for Boston time and one for England. It was getting light now as they crossed over Ireland. You couldn't see anything with the clouds but Martin peered out anyway. There was a five-hour time difference. Clovis would be sound asleep. Probably with Aunt Horty. He wanted to be right there with them. And if Philippa came to his house to go on Aunt Horty's book tour, he'd miss her, too. The stewardess came by and offered him some orange juice. He didn't want it.

"You feeling okay?" she asked, smiling her stewardess smile.

"Sure, I'm okay."

"Anything you want? We have cards, coloring books."

Coloring books? thought Martin. She must think I'm

six. "No, thank you." Martin thought it might be best if he shut his eyes. That way no one tried to foist off cards and comic books on you.

Within an hour the big plane landed smoothly at London's Heathrow Airport and lots of people on the plane applauded. Martin wondered if it was a custom and if the pilot would come out of his cockpit and take a bow.

Martin watched two big black limos draw up to the ramp, and his dad signaled for him and Dorr to get their gear. The stewardess helped Martin with his stuff and the three of them were first off the plane. They didn't have to go through customs. They went right to the limos parked next to the plane. The other people would go on the buses. He knew people were staring at them. Maybe they wondered why they were getting the special treatment. Martin thought he could let them know who they were by shouting, "We're just one big *un*happy family."

Three men took his dad off in one limo and a young man in a tight-fitting coat came up to Dorr.

"I'm Sydney James. I'm going to be one of your father's aides at the Embassy. Ever been in London?"

"Yes," Dorr said, "but not for a long time."

"Then we'll do a roundabout tour and I'll point out the big sights for you." He sat on the jump seat.

As they closed in on London, the man began to point. "There . . . over there . . ."

"Look, Martin, that's Hyde Park Corner. That's where all the political speeches are given."

Poor guy, thought Martin, he doesn't stand a chance with Dorr.

"And there's . . ." Dorr picked it right up. "That's Buckingham Palace. Look, Mart, the flags are flying. That means the Queen is at home."

Their guide looked slightly depressed.

Dorr pointed out Princess Margaret's place. "And this is where Princess Di lives."

At last the guide could score a point. "She's Diana, Princess of Wales, and she now lives at Buckingham Palace."

"That's right." Dorr conceded victory, although she hated to be wrong.

They saw Piccadilly Circus and the Statue of Eros, and Dorr pointed out Harrod's, the famous store. "Do they still have the zoo?"

"They do," the young man said proudly.

The car arrived at Winfield House. They had to be checked in at the huge iron gate and then they drove up a very elegant driveway to the house. It was a big house. Martin didn't think it was as pretty as his own house. Servants bustled out and took their bags. He wondered if Philippa would bite Clovis or ride Clovis.

Their guide tried a new tack. "I say. You don't need a landmark tour. You know London very well. But I wonder if I could show you some out-of-the-way landmarks. What are you doing Saturday night?"

Dorr laughed. "Going on an out-of-the-way tour."

Martin envied Dorr. She didn't miss home one bit.

Chapter 14

Martin wasn't sure it was Dorr who brought Aunt Horty back into his life again, but he thought it might be. He had heard his dad and Dorr talking loudly in his dad's study, and then he heard Dorr in the hall call back to him. "I'm counting on you, Pop. Call her." Then she padded past his room down the hall to her suite. Her rooms were just past his.

Then he heard his dad go into his room. *He must think I'm asleep,* Martin figured, because he hadn't shut his bedroom door. Martin heard him talking to the operator.

"Yes, person to person, please to Hortense Morley."

The whole house was silent. "Is that you, Hortense? I hope I didn't wake you. I'm calling long-distance."

His dad was funny. How else could he have gotten through to her? "Don't be funny. I know everyone in the New World has a telephone."

Martin smiled. Aunt Horty obviously was having her fun with his dad.

"Yes, the reason I called is to tell you we miss you.

59

Yes, we miss you, and we want you to come for a visit. Can you come right away?''

Martin pulled up his covers. In just a little bit Aunt Horty would be here. He hummed, ''Everything's better with Aunt Horty in it.''

Chapter 15

Aunt Horty insisted that they go to the Old English Sheepdog Trials. "We'll see the best of breed. Why settle for a pet shop dog when you can get a blue ribbon baby? *And* your pop is paying."

"I don't want another dog."

"Oh, yes you do!"

Aunt Horty was mad at him. "Martin, you are making me mad. First thing I do is cajole another Clovis out of your dad so we can have some fun, and you act like I'm trying to adopt a cobra for you. Honestly!"

"I have a perfectly good dog at home. Which is where I want to be."

"Cut it out, Martin. We've been all through that. You know, you're a lot like your dad."

"I am not. I'm exactly like my mom."

"Oh, no, you are not! Your mom would never do anything that would make your dad unhappy."

The Sheepdog Trials were held in a school gym. Later, after all the dogs had been chosen from all over the country—from gyms and tents and county halls—the best

61

of the breed would go to Westminster for the big show. Martin could see about twenty-five sheepdogs all prancing about, their trainers and owners brushing up their pets, tying up their topknots so the hair would fall just right when they went in the ring. Martin and Aunt Horty had gone in the back of the ring to watch the trainers. They were funnier than the dogs, but this was serious business for these people. If a dog won best of breed, or even took local ribbons, it added value to the dog's worth and the puppies would be more expensive.

Martin watched the dogs. They were beautiful. Certainly, he never kept Clovis brushed like this. Martin spotted a lady in a long purple knit suit. She had a matching hat laden down with turkey feathers. They blew backwards when she walked her dog. And the dog was a dead ringer for Clovis. The program listed them as No. 74.

''Look, Aunt Horty, there's Clovis!''

''As soon as she's out of the ring we'll head for her booth and see how much she'll take for the dog.''

Despite Martin's disapproval of abandoning Clovis—the real Clovis—he got nudgy about having to wait at all. He watched the turkey feather lady walk her dog and turn him around. The judge cased the dog's jaws and paws and rump and legs. Then he ordered the lady to walk 74 one more time. This time the feather lady turned a corner too abruptly and No. 74 bumped into the judges' card tables. No. 74 knocked two of them over and then hid behind them. No. 74 couldn't seem to find any way out from the tables and the cloths that covered them. The dog kept pushing the tables forward into the ring. The audience laughed with delight. The turkey lady did not find this funny at all and blushed. She had to go in behind the tables and fetch her dog out. Of course, No. 74 was disqualified. The turkey lady stalked out, with dog in tow, to the exit. Martin and Hortense hurried after her.

They found her. She was furious. ''I just can't believe

Syd acted like that. It was very naughty of Syd," she scolded the prancing pup.

"What a beauty," Hortense patted the dog. "You know, we'd love to buy your dog."

"Oh, dear. The dog is not for sale. I just show Syd. Usually just walks off with the prize. Except today, well, today was a disaster."

Aunt Horty went in for the kill. "How much would you take for the dog?"

"I told you, my dear, Syd's just not for sale."

"How old is the pup?" Aunt Horty kept right on.

"Just one year. No, that's not true. Syd's almost two. My, how time flies."

"Same as Clovis," piped up Martin.

The turkey lady gave Hortense a rough time but in the end they made a deal. Syd wasn't cheap. Five hundred American dollars. "It's the breeding, the papers, the lineage, you know. Syd's the best stock. Mother was Bess of Westminster, father was Eton of Staffordshire."

"Will you take a check?" Hortense already had her pen out.

"You'll have to wait a few weeks for Syd. I still have a few commitments to show."

"Well, when?" Hortense handed her the check. "Here, you can fill in your name."

The turkey lady checked out a calendar. "You can pick up Syd on June 15th."

"Perfect," said Hortense. "Just draw us a little map that shows us where you live and how to get there. We'll fetch the dog on June 15th."

Chapter 16

They left the tent and strolled down a narrow street. Hortense pointed out an Olde English Tea Shoppe.

"Come on, Mart, let's 'avva coop." Aunt Horty's cockney accent was pretty good.

"I'd rather have a Seven Up. I don't like the way tea tastes. It's like boiled tree bark."

"Tea is good for you. Better than all that sweet stuff you guzzle."

They crossed the street and headed for the shop.

"Aunt Horty, isn't it just amazing what a dead ringer Syd is for Clovis? Do they have such things as Siamese twin dogs?"

"I don't think so."

"I never saw anything like it," Martin marveled. "Syd's a dead, dead ringer."

The tea shop door had a little bell that alerted everyone in the kitchen that guests had arrived. A very tall, very stiff woman in a crepe dress came from behind the curtain and greeted them.

"Bit of a chill today, isn't there? Can I get you something?"

"Yes, it's very crisp." Hortense smiled at her.

"Full tea or just a cup?"

"Oh, let's have some sandwiches, Martin."

"Okay, but I'd like Seven Up."

Hortense rubbed her hands and studied the little plastic card the hostess/owner/waitress handed her.

"Do you have Seven Up?" Aunt Horty asked for Martin.

"No, madam, this is a tea shop. We have seventeen varieties of tea."

"I'll have the Jasmine, but my young friend likes cold drinks."

"I could make a lemon squash."

"How about that, Martin?"

"Sure, sure." He pulled his chair in to the table.

"Then it's Jasmine and squash. Will you have the scones or sandwiches or both?" She was so serious that Hortense didn't dare look at Martin. They both had that terrible capacity to laugh at ladies like this.

"We'll have everything. We have a lot of business to discuss."

"One tea, sandwiches, scones and a squash." Her face turned lemon sour, and her lips puckered when she said squash. She went to the back of the shop, pulled the curtain aside, went in, pulled the curtain closed, and announced the order although no one was there.

"Don't make me laugh, Martin. You are trying to make me laugh."

"I was not. You are trying to make me."

"Would you be able to tell the dogs apart?"

"I think so, but it would be hard. Too bad we couldn't just buy Syd, then switch him for Clovis. You think we could ever switch them, Aunt Horty?"

Hortense folded her arms and leaned on the table. She

65

was silent for several seconds. Finally she sighed, "I can't think of any way in the world we could do that."

Martin laughed. "I got one idea. Here's how it goes. First we get a big vat of chocolate—like in a chocolate factory. Then we dip Clovis in it."

"That sounds cruel to me. Wouldn't the chocolate be hot?"

"No, it would stick even if it were lukewarm."

"Then what?"

"He'd be a huge chocolate dog. We'd stand him up and put him on a trundle and we'd wheel him out of the chocolate factory."

"Then what?"

"Then we'd put him in Dad's diplomatic pouch and have him delivered right to Dad's desk. We could say it was a birthday present."

"That would be some pouch. More like a body bag, I think."

Martin was impatient. "No, no, Aunt Horty. I'm sure big things can be shipped in diplomatic pouches."

"Okay, so we now have a hardened chocolate dog. Then what?"

"If he got hungry, he could munch on some of the chocolate."

"Sounds cannibalistic to me."

"Aunt Horty, you're being negative."

The curtain clanged back and the proprietress came across the room carrying a tray laden with sandwiches, scones, napkins, cup and saucer, a teapot, and a tall glass with some whitish yellow fluid in it. Martin looked in the glass and swished it about.

"I know. Just eat the sandwiches." Hortense handed the plate to Martin. He took two and picked the top piece of bread off both.

"Don't *do* that, Martin. The lady is watching."

"It's got brown toothpaste in it."

66

"That's anchovy paste. Very good. Nibble. Just eat the bread. So what happens when the chocolate dog arrives in your father's office?"

"Dad would call and invite us over for chocolate."

"Dreamer." Hortense sipped her tea. She bit into one of the sandwiches and returned it quickly to the plate. "You're right. That is brown toothpaste."

Martin laughed

"Sorry, I interrupted." She gulped her tea to wash down the bite of sandwich.

"Okay, here's another idea. How do you like this one?"

"I'm waiting."

"We roll Clovis up and put him in the spare tire compartment of a Rolls. I saw that once in a movie. They smuggled in diamonds and all sorts of things."

"Do we fly in the car or bring it by boat?"

"Guess we'd have to fly. Clovis would be a donut after six days in a tire at sea."

Hortense eked out more tea by winding the tea bag around her spoon and adding hot water.

"What if we drugged the dog and I wore him in as a coat?"

"Not bad. But you *know* Clovis would yawn just as you passed the customs man. One of his big huge long yawns where you see all his molars."

"There ought to be a way, Mart. We need James Bond and his bag of tricks *and* his car."

"I don't see why we can't switch Syd for Clovis. It ought to be a cinch. They do it every night on TV."

"I'm game. But where? There are customs at every port and every point of entry to Britain. Especially at airports."

"Even the small ones?"

"The jets don't land on the small runways."

"Couldn't we get a small plane? Like the one Lindbergh used to cross the ocean? Small planes can fly under radar. They never get noticed."

"And if you got caught, what then?"

"I don't even want to think about it. Hasn't anyone ever beat the rap and brought an animal into England?"

"Sure. Lots of people have tried. Famous people. But they don't keep the pet long. Back it goes to the US."

Martin watched his aunt wrap several of the toothpaste sandwiches in a napkin and tuck them in her bag. They ate the ham ones.

"What are you going to do with the sandwiches, Aunt Horty?"

"I'm taking them. I don't want to hurt the lady's feelings." She waved for the check.

"I have just one tiny thought. And mind you it's tiny." She moved over and whispered in Martin's ear.

Martin's eyes widened and he nodded his head affirmatively. Then he turned and looked Hortense straight in the eye.

"That's genius, Aunt Horty, just plain genius."

They paid their check and waved goodbye to the Olde English Lady.

Chapter 17

Martin knew very well that Aunt Horty was having second thoughts about the Clovis Caper. That's what he had tagged it. Hortense kept reiterating that in no way would they be breaking the law if they exchanged dogs far enough out at sea. "We won't even see a customs man."

Now she was definitely getting cold feet. Martin coaxed Dorr to help.

"The two of you are stark raving mad!" Dorr's comment didn't help Martin's morale. Nevertheless, Martin was persistent. Finally, Dorr agreed to see if she could find some freighter timetables. When she got into the project, she also found out all kinds of things they needed to know. There *was* a boat that left Boston and came directly to Portsmouth. Dorr had asked around. The boat was called *S.S. Peaches*. The captain was not well-liked. From what she could gather from other seamen in Portsmouth, he had already had a few run-ins with the law.

"I don't know, Mart. I think you and Aunt Horty are treading very questionable ground. This guy sounds freaky."

Aunt Horty took the opposite view. "I'd rather deal

with a guy who's been a bit naughty than with some God-fearing churchman turned sailor. Look, when's the next time his boat is due in Portsmouth?''

Dorr consulted her notes and the schedule. ''This Saturday around noon.''

''What say we drive there and meet him? It's only a few hours drive. We'll take a look-see and then make our decision. The *S.S. Peaches?*'' Aunt Horty shook her head. ''What a name for a boat.''

''Wait till you see the boat. It might be a great name for it.''

''Is there a decent map of England in this place?'' Dorr asked.

Martin knew his tutor had one. He raced down the hall to the library where he did his homework. He got the map and raced back. ''Here,'' he said. ''Let's look.'' He spread the map out.

They were so engrossed in checking out where the feather lady lived and where the freighter would dock that they didn't even hear the professor come in.

''Going somewhere?'' Martin's dad asked, peering at the map on the table.

''What are you doing here, John? We thought you'd be gone till tomorrow?'' Hortense said smoothly. Then she tried to fold the map carefully so she'd have a moment to get her wits together. ''Yes, we're looking for a crater where we could have a meal.''

''The best craters in England are right out on the road in front.'' He eyed the group suspiciously.

Hortense was making an absolute mess of the map, and handed it to Dorr, who handed it to Martin, who handed it back to his aunt.

Martin's dad took the map from her and carefully opened it and refolded it properly. ''Now where's that new beast?''

''He's still in the country, Dad. Just wait till you see him. He's Clovis cloned.''

70

"Then I assume that you are going to call it Clonis?"

They all moaned.

"His name is Syd, Dad."

"Change it. My aide is Syd. We can't have the dog called Syd. It would be insulting. So when do you get the dog?"

"It's complicated. We found exactly the dog we want. And you should have seen the turkey lady."

"Hortense, have you completely lost your mind? First you talk about craters and now a turkey lady." John Prentiss was having a good time. He sat down and arranged his body comfortably. He was going to stay awhile.

"The lady who has Syd, Dad, she's the turkey lady."

Hortense recouped her cool. "You see, John, we were all surprised to see you. We thought you'd be gone a few days, and suddenly you are here."

"Yes, well, my meeting broke up early. So here I am. Now, what about the turkey lady?"

Aunt Horty did an imitation of the turkey lady walking Syd that made Martin's dad laugh.

"She took little mincing steps like this." Hortense walked the length of the room pulling an immense, imaginary dog. "And didn't the dog do just what our Clovis would have done? Knocked over the judges' table, then got confused and couldn't get out from under the table. That was that. Syd was *dis*qualified."

"You purchased a disqualified dog?"

"Listen, she didn't want to sell it."

"So where is it and how much?"

"She has two more shows to do, Dad, then we can have Syd. We just have to go pick Syd up. She lives in the country. That's why we were studying the map."

"How much, Hortense?"

"Five." Hortense seemed uncomfortable. "I'll split it if that seems a bit much."

"Five what?"

"Five hundred."

"Five hundred what?"

"Dollars. Didn't I say that?"

"You could buy a horse for that."

"But I don't want a horse, Dad."

"What do you think Clovis is?"

"A sheepdog, Dad. There were twenty-five or so dogs there. It was something to see. It would have killed you."

"I've no doubt of that." John Prentiss studied the map. "So were you able to find the turkey lady and her dog?"

"Yes, we did," Hortense enunciated each word. "Actually, we thought we might make a weekend of it. Go on Saturday morning, have a picnic, stay in a charming inn, come back Sunday. Don't you think that sounds like fun?"

"I certainly do. Count me in. But don't forget that it's *this* Saturday night I'm having a reception. You all must be there. You do have a dress, don't you, Hortense?"

"Yes, indeed, I have several quite stunning tribal dresses. I'll wear something with porcupine quills stitched in. Stop 'em dead fashion."

"I know you will do just that." The professor grinned, looked at his watch. "Oh, oh, I must make some calls. See you later."

Hortense looked at Dorr. Dorr looked at Martin. Martin looked worried. "What will we do if Dad decides to come too?"

"Don't worry, honey, he just talks big." Hortense gave him a pat on the shoulder. But it wasn't a very convincing pat.

"Holy cow," Martin moaned. "Doesn't anything ever go smoothly around here? Now we have something else to worry about."

Chapter 18

As it was, Martin had nothing to worry about. His dad was snowed under with paperwork. Delighted, they left him a note and promised they'd be home in plenty of time for his party.

There was little or no traffic on the A3 and they made it to the coast long before the *S.S. Peaches* sidled into her berth. Once they'd made their deal, they were going to zip over to Torquay and find out about renting a boat.

"Okay, Martin. Here's the plan." Aunt Horty ticked off the steps. "You go on board as soon as the boat docks. We'll wait till the customs are aboard too. Chances are the crew will be cleared first, and they'll leave. The captain and his mate will wait till they get clearance for their cargo. See if you can find out which one is the captain, and don't approach him till he's left the customs men. Then speak up and tell him exactly what you want."

"And what exactly do I want, Aunt Horty?" Martin felt nervous about the whole thing and wished that Aunt Horty would do the bargaining.

"Oh, for heaven's sake. You know very well. Just don't

tip your hand about the dogs too soon. Meanwhile, we'll wait right down here at the pier. If he gets tough, give a yell. I just think he's more likely to feel sorry for a little boy than he will for two old crones.''

"I am not a little boy!" Martin said firmly.

"And I am not an old crone!" Dorr added. "Speak for yourself, Horty.''

Martin's hands were sweating. The back of his tee shirt clung to him. It was a hot, muggy day. He climbed up the ramp and cased the ship. It was a big ship but run-down, rusty, and Martin guessed it was pretty old. The low part of the freighter was so heavy with cargo it practically sat on the water. Martin wondered how on earth they managed to keep the cargo from floating away when the weather was bad. But then he saw that everything was securely strapped and covered with a heavy tarp. The customs agents walked up and down the narrow aisle and checked off packages on their declaration sheet. Martin thought that this was a real tramp steamer. He wondered if it ever carried passengers, but from the look of the crew and the cargo he would say it probably didn't. Tramps, he knew, were free to go wherever they could make a good buck. However, the *S.S. Peaches* seemed to be on a regular schedule to and from Boston. It was the only one that called at Portsmouth. This ship had no exotic wares from Martinique or Mozambique. He spied a man in chino pants and jacket toting what looked like a gym case.

"Are you the captain of the *S.S. Peaches?*''

"No, thank God, I am not.''

This guy had a British accent. Martin had never given a thought to the fact they might have to deal with a Brit. That wouldn't be good news.

"Do you know where I can find him, please?''

"What do you want with him?''

"Oh, it's personal.''

The man in chinos looked at the serious boy and thought

74

it pretty funny. He wondered if the kid had run away from home and was looking for a hitch.

He looked down at the cargo area. "See that man down there in the dark green jacket? That's him. That's Captain Nicholson."

"Thanks," Martin said politely and started to climb down. He saw that Captain Nicholson wore mirror sunglasses against the water glare. He had a beard that looked to Martin at least three days old. In fact, Martin thought a bath was in order. The man also didn't look like he was in the best of humor. Martin waited till he got closer. The guy in the chino pants watched and shouted, "Captain Nick, someone to see you about a personal matter." He pointed to Martin.

Nicholson walked toward Martin. He really was dirty. Despite his muscular build he had a potbelly.

"What do you want? I'm busy." He waved "shove-off" to the chino pants man. Then he stared down at Martin. "So?"

"Well," Martin cleared his throat. "I'm here with my aunt and sister, and we want to hire you."

"What do you think I am, a charter cruiser? Where's your family?"

"Down there." Martin pointed.

Nicholson leaned over the railing and gave Martin a wicked grin. "Not bad. Not bad. Which is which?"

Martin knew that Dorr would be furious and Aunt Horty delighted. "The one in the orange pants is my aunt."

"Not a bad dish to put before the king."

Martin wondered what on earth he was talking about.

"Come on, let's join the girls."

"No, first you have to do business with me."

"*You?* You think I'm going to do business with a kid?"

Martin ignored him, swallowed hard, and spilled out his message.

"We are looking for a trustworthy seaman to carry some

75

cargo for us from Boston to here and then pick up the same kind of cargo here and take it back to Boston. We'll make all the arrangements at both ends so it will go like clockwork.''

Nicholson peered meanly at Martin. "What's the cargo?''

"Just a small crate.''

"Why don't you just mail a small crate?''

"We can't. It's special.''

"Boy, this is a new twist,'' Nicholson said disgustedly. "Send in a kid to do a man's job. Let's go meet the leader.''

Martin was dejected. He would have liked to pull his own weight on this trip. They walked back up the steps and down the ramp to Hortense and Dorr. Martin said, "This is Captain Nicholson. He wanted to meet you.''

Hortense gave the captain one look. There were no nice hellos or handshakes. "Did he tell you what we need?''

"To some degree.'' Nicholson rubbed his stubbled chin. "What he didn't let on is what he wants me to carry.''

"He didn't tell you about our itty-bitty dog?''

Dorr chimed in. "We want to bring one dog from Boston, and we are going to give you one to take right back there. Kind of a round-trip package.''

"So you want to switch dogs. That it?''

They all looked guilty. "That's it.'' Aunt Horty reddened.

"Forget it! I thought maybe you were into something interesting.''

"When you see our crate, you may think we are.''

"What's the gimmick? You stuff the hound with diamonds? In one end, out the other?''

"Hardly,'' Dorr said sarcastically. "If that were the case, you'd get the loot, wouldn't you?''

"That's true.'' Nicholson took his hands out of his pockets and folded them in front of him carefully, snapping each knuckle as he did.

76

"You two dames want to go dancing tonight? I can get a pal."

Martin was outraged. Here they had come to do legitimate business and Captain Nicholson was asking Aunt Horty for a date. "They can't go," Martin said sternly. "We have to get back to London."

"Too bad. We could have had a good time. So what *do* you do? Stitch stuff in their coats?"

"No, we do not stitch stuff in their coats," Aunt Horty said. "We don't want to stitch. We want to switch. I give you one dog in Boston. You bring it here. We give you the same kind of dog here. You take it there. The dogs are identical."

"Listen, lady." He focused his shades on Hortense. "I don't care if your dogs are dead ringers for each other. Smuggling dogs into England is bad news. Don't ask. Don't even think about it."

"I'm not asking for anything. I'm willing to pay the freight with a bonus. And *you* don't smuggle anything. We never see a port. We'll rendezvous with you at sea. Outside the twelve-mile-limit. That's not smuggling as I see it." Hortense was out of breath.

"And just how are you three dodos going to meet me at sea?"

"We're first-rate sailors." Hortense said proudly. "We've been sailing all our lives."

"Where, on some lake in Wisconsin?"

"No, off Cape Cod and Nantucket and Bar Harbor and the Vineyard. We know what we're doing."

"Yeah, we're good." Martin said.

Nicholson roared with laughter.

"This is the damndest thing I have ever heard."

"Look," said Dorr, "you're not the only one in the world who can run a boat. I'll bet I could ace you in a race any day. You tell us where we can meet you. Pick it out on this nautical map. We'll be there when you're there.

Our man in Boston meets you on your next trip. You pick up our cargo. We meet you out there,'' she pointed toward the ocean, ''and we make the switch. Easy as pie.''

Martin knew that if they actually made the deal today they were going to get Mrs. Grant to get Clovis to the freighter. Why was Dorr calling Mrs. Grant ''our man''?

''Look, kids, go get the car. We're in a meter zone. Let me finish up the deal with the captain.''

Dorr and Martin knew that Aunt Horty was going to barter. She had finally gotten the turkey lady down a hundred dollars. And she told Martin she could have done better except that they had to get going. Martin just stayed put, and Dorr went for the car.

Aunt Horty zeroed in. ''So, how much for the whole job?''

''How about a thou?''

''You're off your rocker, that's twice what the dog cost.''

''No way will I do it for less.''

''How about five?''

''Pounds or dollars?''

''Dollars for heaven's sake. Pounds is almost the thou.''

''Lady, I don't even want to do this. Pay what I want or forget it.'' He looked like he meant it.

''Oh, all right. Five hundred pounds.''

''Up front. The whole wad.''

''What kind of fool do you take me for? You get 10 percent now. You get 80 percent when we switch. And you get the rest when you deliver the cargo to Boston.'' She reached for her check book. ''Who gets it, the *S.S. Peaches*?''

''No, stupid, me. J. Nicholson.''

Hortense scratched out the check. She was furious. Her pride in bargaining was wounded.

He scanned the check. ''This better be good.''

"What do you care? You have the hostages at both ends."

Dorr had driven the car right up to the wharf. Hortense was watching the captain mark the map. "There, right there. Watch out for the lighthouse on the way out. Don't go near it."

They walked down to the car. Nicholson held the check between his thumb and forefinger like he might hold a bad fish. He helped Hortense into the car. "There you go."

Hortense pried his hand off her elbow. "Okay. You pick up the cargo in Boston."

"I told you before," he snarled. "Have your man at Moran's pier in Boston at midnight on the fourth. Can you remember that?"

"Right. And we'll see you on the sixteenth at ten sharp."

Martin watched Nicholson's wicked grin. He sure didn't trust that gink. He rolled down the window. "Hey, Captain, what backup plan do we have if we miss the boat?"

Nicholson peered in at Martin. "If we miss each other I go right into port and the mutt goes right in the drink."

They all sat there with their mouths open. "What a rotten thing to do! I don't want you on this case. Aunt Horty, get your check back!"

"Oh, come on kid, cool it. I was just teasing. You guys are real touchy. Look, if by some goof-up you miss me, you'll find me right here. I'll keep the dog hidden. Then we'll switch on the way out. Okay?"

"You *will* be there?" Hortense sounded skeptical.

"Honey, where you're involved, you can count on it."

Dorr stepped on the gas and they streaked off down the pier. "What a creep."

"Was he trying to pick you up, Aunt Horty?"

"I suppose you could say that."

Martin could not see Aunt Horty out on the town with

the captain. He leaned back in the seat and tried to picture it.

"Well, we made it through stage one. We'll beat this game after all."

Martin felt queasy. What if they didn't beat it? What if they got caught? What would his dad do? He'd lose his job and Martin knew that his dad loved his job. Much as he wanted Clovis in England, he really had to ask himself if it was worth this worry. But Hortense had started a project and Martin knew that once Aunt Horty was in to something, she stuck with it. After all, she *had* taught her chimp to type.

Chapter 19

The little harbor at Torquay had several boat rental places. The biggest one was Binn's. Hortense shoved Martin out of the car and down the steps into the office which was a small lean-to on a pier. "Ask!"

Martin peered in at an elderly man. "Are you in charge here?"

"Haven't a boat today, as you may have noticed."

Martin thought the man had the biggest Adam's apple he'd ever seen. "That's okay. We came to reserve a boat for early on the morning of June sixteenth. Can we do that?"

"I suppose you can. But I don't think I could let you skipper by yourself."

"Aunt Horty, please come down here!" Martin was exasperated with her. She was making him do all the leg work, and she knew very well that eventually she'd have to rescue him.

Hortense crushed into the shed beside Martin. "I'm Hortense Morley and this young man is my nephew. We need a fairly good-sized fishing boat for the sixteenth of June. We're going fishing.''

"Got a nice little boat for ladies.''

"We don't *want* a nice boat for ladies. We want something that sleeps four, with plumbing. We want to do some real fishing.''

"You going to have a skipper?''

"*I* am the skipper.''

"What you desire, madam, is a lot of boat for a woman to handle.''

"Please, Mr. . . .'' She paused for him to supply her with a name.

"Binn. Harold Binn.''

"You own this place?''

"Sure do.''

"Mr. Binn, we're all good sailors. There would be three of us. We have handled all kinds of boats: Evinrude, Volvo, Penta, Newport, Stingray. We've all been to sea since we were kids. My dad taught me how to sail. So don't worry.''

"Got to worry. Insurance is mighty steep.''

"If you promise to hold a good-sized boat for us, we'll be by the night of the fifteenth. We're going to stay at the hotel here. Then early on the sixteenth we want to go fishing.''

"Don't hold boats without a down payment.''

"Here, let me,'' Dorr said. "How much is it?''

"Fifty for the day.'' Dorr blanched.

"I don't have that much cash on me. Will you take a check?''

"No, no, afraid not. No checks from Americans.''

"*My* check is on a British bank,'' Dorr snapped back.

"Got to be frank. Don't like any checks. Just paper.''

Among the three of them they almost had enough. "How about taking thirty eight pounds?''

"Aunt Horty, we need gas money,'' Martin warned.

She removed a five pound note from the pile.

Binn said sadly, "Look, I don't mean to put you on the spot, but I do get stuck with bum paper. My wife has laid down the law. No more checks. Just give me a check for the remainder and I'll hope your word is good. I'll hold the *Torquay* for you for the sixteenth. We open at six A.M."

"Now this does have a toilet and bunks?"

"Got a picture of her right here." Binn pulled open his desk drawer and rummaged about. "Here. Here she is."

Hortense took the photo and studied it. "Yes, she's fine."

Martin tilted to get a view. "Boy, what a boat!"

His reaction reactivated Binn's suspicions. "Too big for you, eh?"

Hortense drew up to her full height. "No, we were wondering if this was the biggest boat you had."

Chapter 20

Mrs. Grant was so delighted to hear Martin's voice and talk to him that she didn't realize what she'd agreed to do until she'd hung up.

"Mrs. Grant, it's Martin. How are you? I sure miss you."

She told him everything. How Clovis missed him. What mean tricks Charlotte still played on him now that she could say chocolate chip. "You can just imagine that! First she just shouted 'Clovis, come get youh dinnah!' Now she gets him everytime on cookies."

After a report on the Embassy and Embassy life, Martin got up the courage to ask his favor. "Can you buy a big carrier of some kind at a pet store and put Clovis in it and take him to Moran's pier on the night of June fourth? I will have a man meet you there at midnight."

"Midnight? Did you say midnight? Why then?"

Martin didn't want to be too specific about why they had to keep this exchange very quiet. "Well, there are no people loading boats at that hour and the freight captain can take Clovis on board then.

"Aunt Horty thought you should go see Dr. Griffin and ask him to give you some tranquilizers for Clovis. Then he'll sleep all night. The boat leaves the next morning at dawn."

"Martin, am I hearing right? You want me to take your dog to a pier at midnight, in a big case, and give him to a strange man? How will I get there?"

"Can you use your car, Mrs. Grant? I'll pay you back for the gas. And Clovis loves your car."

"Well, is this captain going to haul my car up on his boat?"

"No, no. Clovis should be knocked out by then from the pills. All you have to do is get Clovis and his case as far as the pier. Then the captain will help you lift him out, and put him on the boat. Will you do that for me? I don't trust anyone else."

Mrs. Grant laughed after she hung up. Trust anyone else. There *was* no one else nutty enough to do this job. She looked at Clovis. "How did I ever agree to get into this crazy mess?"

The pet store didn't have anything in the way of a pet carrier that Clovis would fit into. Nor did the pet department at Filene's. The salesman there suggested a crate. "What I need is something about the size of a trunk but flexible," Mrs. Grant explained.

"Well, we have big hampers. Maybe the luggage department would have a tailgate basket." The salesman was trying to be helpful.

"What's a tailgate basket?"

"It's for people who go to games and matches in their station wagons. They flop down the back and have a buffet. The case is equipped with all the gear." He went in the store room and came out with a huge wicker basket.

"It's big!" Mrs Grant admired it. She lifted it. "It's heavy. What's in there?"

He opened the case. They both studied the gear: plates, glasses, knives, forks, thermos.

"I don't need all that stuff. I'll send along some dog chow and some cookies and I'm sure they'll give him water."

"You planning on putting a body in there?"

"I guess you could say that. But I don't need all this stuff. I just want the basket."

"It comes with the basket. You can strip it when you get home. But it's one deal."

"Okay, I'll take it. I can use it sometime in case the family ever does anything normal like go on a picnic." She handed the man her charge card.

"Should I send it?"

"No," Mrs. Grant smiled. "I'll just eat it right here."

Chapter 21

Martin slipped into his velvet blazer. He wore a new silk shirt his aunt had bought for him at Harrod's. He polished the toes of his shoes on the back of his plaid trousers. He felt good. He had never worn an outfit like this. He stood tiptoe to get a good look. The mirrors in the whole house were on the insides of closet doors, but unless you were six feet six, you would never see below your waist. Martin jumped up and down. He thought he really looked neat.

He walked down the hall to Hortense's quarters. He tapped on the door.

"Come in," Hortense called.

Martin peered in. He saw she was fastening a slender chain on her neck. She wore a low-cut, black, slinky dress. She looked like a movie star.

"Aunt Horty," Martin said admiringly. "You look just fabulous."

"You like my tribal outfit?"

"It's swell. Just wait till Dad sees you."

"I think he's scared to death I might show up in a

hand-painted mu-mu with beaded headdress and a dead chicken.''

Martin fingered the large stone around Hortense's neck. "Is that real?"

"Yep, been in the family for years and years. It'll be yours some day. It's a lovely diamond, really."

"I can't wear a diamond, Aunt Horty. I'm a boy."

"You'll meet a lovely girl, and you'll have her engagement ring right in the vault."

"Oh, yuk. If I had to marry someone like Saucey Sanders, I'd give up."

"You'll change and so will Saucey. Come on, honey, we'd better go."

Martin escorted Hortense into the ballroom. It was the first time he'd seen the house all filled with people. The chandeliers glittered, the candles glowed, men in knickered uniforms passed champagne. There were trays of food everywhere. He spied his dad chatting with a man wearing a kilt and steered Hortense over toward him.

The man in the kilt saw Hortense first. "I say, John, who is that?"

Martin and Hortense came toward them. "That's Hortense Morley, my sister-in-law." He said this with a tone of pride.

"*The* Hortense Morley? The author and anthropologist?"

"The same one. And that's my son with her."

There were introductions. "Hortense, you look wonderful," John Prentiss said with awe. Martin had never seen his father so impressed.

"Hortense, let's have a dance before I'm swamped." His dad left Martin with the kilt man. Martin wondered what you said to a man in a skirt. Do you wear skirts on the street? What's the big pouch?

Martin was glad to see Dorr. He felt like he'd been rescued from the Scots. "Do forgive me if I take my brother away for a moment."

88

"Thanks, Dorr. I was running out of kilt talk."

"I wanted you to get a gander at Aunt Horty and Dad dancing it up. You won't believe it."

Martin scanned the floor. There was his dad laughing and smiling and holding Aunt Horty very, very close.

"They're hitting it off a lot better than they used to, don't you think, Mart?"

Before Martin could answer, a young man in a British army outfit asked Dorr to dance. She left, reluctantly. "I'll be right back. Keep your eyes open."

Martin walked to the side of the dance floor. To look busy he took two of the canapés from a tray. He popped one in his mouth and held the other. And he held the one in his mouth for as long as he could. He was desperate for somewhere to spit it out. To his relief, he found a large palm.

"Your son does not like smoked salmon," observed Hortense. "And it's sooooooo expensive."

"How do you know that?" The professor held Hortense a bit away so he could talk to her.

"Because he just spit a large piece of it into one of your palm trees."

"What appalling manners!" They both laughed.

Martin looked around for something to eat that would get rid of the taste. Disgustedly he eyed the trays. If you didn't get the pink stuff, you got grey beads, or worse, the brown toothpaste. Couldn't they ever serve nice ham sandwiches with mustard or a hot dog?

"Eyeing the delicacies?" It was Dorr back from her twirl.

"Forget it. They're awful." He watched her put a big plop of grey beads on a melba round and pop it into her mouth. "Ahhhhhhhh." She crunched. "Marvelous."

Martin looked away. He spotted his aunt and his dad heading toward them.

"Thanks for the dance, Hortense. You're great!"

"Oh, I'm a klutz, but your party is smashing. Except, of course, for the salmon."

"Well," Martin's dad said, "I'll have to do a better spread for the sixteenth."

"What's happening on the sixteenth, Dad?" Martin said. There was just a touch of worry in his voice.

"The Queen—*the* Queen—has agreed to come to tea here. I didn't think I'd even get on her calendar this season. We'll really have to turn on the glamour."

"Does it have to be that day?" Martin asked. Aunt Horty gave him a "cool it" look.

"Do you think that *I* tell the Queen when to come? She tells you when she's coming. You ought to know that."

The professor studied the group. He was no dummy at reading faces. "Why, what's the matter with the sixteenth? Surely you have nothing more important to do than meet the Queen, do you?"

Hortense gave him one of her lovelier smiles. "We were going to pick up Clonis. We thought we'd drive down on the fifteenth and come right back on the sixteenth. Don't worry, we'll be back long before the Queen arrives. Isn't tea at four?"

"You cannot go. That's that. She expects to meet my family, and I expect my family to be at my side. If you had car trouble, well, we just can't take that chance."

"But we must go, John. It's the only day for months the turkey lady can meet us. It's just a hop, skip, and a jump away."

"Well then, do your hop, skip, and jump on the fifteenth."

Martin could see his dad was getting mad. It was just like the time his dad said he had the job. His dad had the Queen coming, and they were off to the turkey lady's place, and then on to Mr. Binn's boat to make the big switch. If his dad ever knew he'd kill them. He tried to feign a yawn and leaned against one of the gold ballroom chairs.

"Look, Martin, you can cut out now if you'd like. I'll talk this over with your aunt. Oh, incidentally, I had a call from Terry Tellison. Remember him?"

Martin wanted to say, "I'll never forget him."

"Well, he's in London and he's going to have lunch with me. I thought you'd like to come along."

"Sure, Dad. Well, if it's okay, I'm going to turn in."

His Aunt Horty handed him a napkin. "Here, Mart, do take some salmon with you. Just fold up the napkin and slip in as many slices as you like. If you're hungry later, you'll be glad to have it."

Martin gave her a dirty look. She must have seen him get rid of his fish. Boy, did she ever have an eagle eye.

He left the crowded room and moved on quietly to his rooms. "Wow, this is just what we need now," he muttered. "A visit from the Queen." Martin wondered if this streak of bad luck would jinx the whole operation.

Chapter 22

Mrs. Grant read the directions on the bottle of pills. Charlotte aped her by counting in Spanish. "Uno, dos, tres, cuatro," she screamed. She *could* go to ciento.

"Please, Charlotte, alto!"

Charlotte frolicked up and down her perch, preening her wings out into a gorgeous fan of blue and green.

Mrs. Grant got down on her knees and pulled Clovis over to her. She pushed the pills into Clovis's mouth and held his snout firmly closed. Clovis resisted as much as he could but Mrs. Grant had a first-rate hammerlock on him. Finally he wiggled frantically and Mrs. Grant let him go. He shook his head furiously. Clovis did not like swallowing anything but chocolate chip cookies.

"There now, that wasn't so bad. I'm going out to the car now with the basket. By the time I get back you ought to be in dreamland."

But when she got back to the kitchen there was Clovis greeting her warmly.

Clovis seemed to be quite ready for a long walk and followed Mrs. Grant everywhere she went. "Listen, fellow, you got to go to sleep." She checked her watch. That dog wasn't about to turn in.

"Well, come on then, we'll get going. Maybe you'll zonk out on the way to the dock."

After asking directions from at least three people, Mrs. Grant finally found the right pier. She was early.

Clovis paced around her, fascinated with these new surroundings and the smell of water.

"That's your cruise ship over there!" Mrs. Grant pointed to the bobbing hulk of the *S.S. Peaches*. "Don't envy you any going on that barge."

She sat on the front seat of her Chevy, keeping both the doors on the passenger side open. Clovis wanted to run.

"I think the doctor got it all wrong. He sent you uppers instead of downers. You want to play and I want to fall asleep sitting here."

"That you, Grant?" Mrs. Grant peered around the car. She didn't see a soul. Then in a second the voice was directly in front of her and she could make out the silhouette of a man.

"Dear Lord, you scared me out of what little wits I have left."

Nicholson didn't care one whit and she knew it. He took a look at the wildly playful, very much awake Clovis. The dog was trying to evaluate the newcomer. Should he like him or not?

"Sit down, Clovis!" The dog sat.

"This is the itsy-bitsy little thing I'm carting?"

"He's an old sweetheart."

"I thought old sweetheart was supposed to be in a carrier sound asleep."

"Beats me. I gave him his three knock-out pills. He's probably going to fall down in a minute."

"Well, come on, we can board. I'll stow him in my cabin. Saves us having to lift him. Then how's about having a little drink with me?"

93

Mrs. Grant patted Clovis's head. "You be good, boy, and write when you get work." She handed Nicholson the tailgate case.

"What the devil am I supposed to do with this?"

"It's got his food and jam-jams in it."

"You *got* to be kidding. You think this thing will hold this mutt?"

"The man at the store said it would hold one hundred fifty pounds. Besides, Clovis is mostly fur."

"Well, if the bottom falls out of this plan, it will be your neck, not mine."

"Don't you worry about my neck. If Ms. Hortense gets mad, worry about yours."

"Tell me. Why would anyone *want* that?" He pointed at Clovis as he shoved the dog into his cabin. "I'll never have an answer."

As soon as they left, Clovis put up a real yowl. There was one man on watch. He hadn't seen Mrs. Grant or the captain come on board since he'd been in the kitchen getting his fifth cup of coffee. But as he headed back to the ramp he heard Clovis yelp. The noise seemed to come from the captain's cabin. What kind of monkey business was this? He went to take a look.

Clovis had tried everything to escape from the small cabin. He had pawed the door, yelped, and bayed. He had tried to get out the porthole window but couldn't reach it. When he heard footsteps outside the cabin, he slipped behind the door. As the mate came in to look around with his flashlight, Clovis slipped right out, ran down the deck and down the ramp and down the pier and down the street. Clovis was heading home.

The mate couldn't find anything that would account for yelping. "I must be losing my grip. I would have sworn I heard barking."

94

Chapter 23

Mrs. Grant had stopped for a few things at an all-night supermarket. She felt hungry and realized that she hadn't had a bite to eat since breakfast. Dr. Griffin had called with the vet's name and her first stop had been the vet's office for Clovis's tranquilizers. After that she had shopped for dry dog food and chocolate chip cookies. Then she had to find Clovis's old blanket to line the picnic basket with so he'd feel at home. Now that she had accomplished all this, and Clovis was probably sound asleep on the *Peaches*, she was going to put the car away, make a sandwich, and maybe have a cold beer. She pulled into the driveway and looked up at the lighted porch.

"I do not believe my eyes. Do not *believe* my eyes. I am hallucinating."

Sitting smack in the middle of the front stoop was none other than Clovis. Home from the pier. And Clovis was overjoyed to see her.

"Well, come on into the kitchen." She sat down and patted Clovis. He wanted to be loved and played with. "I got to think, baby. What on earth am I going to do? You have missed the boat!''

Clovis panted and wiggled. "Okay, I'll get some water for you.''

When she put his bowl down, she saw the pills on the rug. Clovis had spit them out. "No wonder you never got sleepy. You never even swallowed one pill." She picked up the sticky mess with a paper towel and tossed it out. Then she hurried to the cupboard, and pulled out some cookies. "This time, old boy, you are going to get those pills down and keep them down." She pulled out a handful of cookies. Clovis went wild, wagging his tail and moaning for joy. Mrs. Grant pried out some of the chocolate chips and stuck in the tranquilizers. She made Clovis sit up and beg. He wolfed down the cookies.

And the pills worked. Fast. Mrs. Grant had to drag Clovis to the car. It was already beginning to get light. She ran back into the house to the storeroom. There was a large basket of old clothes waiting to go to the Salvation Army. She'd put Clovis in the bottom of the basket and when she got to the pier, she'd pile on the old clothes. Clovis couldn't have cared less about being shoved into the basket. He just sank down and slept.

She put her foot on the gas and headed back to the pier. The sun was coming up just as she got there and she saw that the *S.S. Peaches* had already pulled up to the ramp. She stopped the car and jumped out and waved a pair of polka-dot shorts at Nicholson, who was on the top deck giving orders.

"Captain Nicholson, wait. WAIT!''

Nicholson whistled to the crew to hold everything. He put up his hand. He could not believe what he saw. There was the mad black lady from last night. They had had a nice talk but he couldn't get her to join him for a drink. He'd had a few anyway and wished now that he hadn't. His head ached. He knew very well why she was back.

96

That damned dog had escaped from his cabin. But why was she waving shorts at him?

"Captain, you forgot your laundry." Mrs. Grant had run to the boat and was out of breath.

The crew thought this was pretty funny. One guy shouted, "I never knew you washed anything, Captain."

Nicholson ran down the ramp and hustled over to Mrs. Grant. "I can't take that pooch on now," he whispered. "Too many people. He escaped. What could I do? What do you expect me to do now?"

"I expect you to help me get that basket in my car into your cabin. If you act cool, man, no one will be the wiser."

The crew gathered on deck to watch. They saw Nicholson and the black lady carefully bring out a basket of clothes from the back seat of her car.

"Lord God, Captain, don't let it tip or the treasure asleep in there will fall out," Mrs. Grant warned Nicholson.

Nicholson wasn't feeling strong enough to object to her bossing him around. They split the weight of the basket between them and climbed the ramp.

"All right, guys, get back to work. It's no big deal. Just my stuff."

They couldn't help hearing Mrs. Grant scolding him.

"You went off without your clean clothes and you went off without paying me. You owe me thirty dollars *and* carfare."

Nicholson's mouth opened. "Thirty dollars!"

"You haven't paid me in months."

Nicholson knew it was a diversionary joke but he didn't think it was funny when she insisted he pay her. They stowed Clovis in the cabin and he hurried her off the deck.

She was not about to be hurried. "Thirty dollars, please."

He pulled his wallet out and handed her the money. She quickly went down the ramp, then turned and shouted "I pick up your dirty stuff when you return, right?"

"Right. Same place."

Mrs. Grant leaned on her car. "This was what is known as a photo finish," she panted. "I'm getting too old for this!" She watched the *Peaches* till it left the harbor. Then she headed home. She had one more chore to do.

"Person to person to Martin Prentiss." The operator ordered up Martin in London.

His curious voice connected with her. "Hello, hello, who is this?"

"This is your man in Boston. The goods are on the way."

Chapter 24

Martin couldn't believe the turkey lady. After all the phone calls and chatting, she didn't want to sell them Syd.

"I tell you I can't part with Syd. Syd is part of me. I know it's psychological, but I can't help it. I simply cannot sell my Syd."

Aunt Horty was furious. "Look, we have already paid you for Syd. You cashed my check. You *have* sold us the dog."

Martin checked his watch. It was getting close to four. They still had a couple of hours drive to get to Torquay. They'd be lucky if they made it before dark. And the boat yard would be closed for sure. What if the boat was totally wrong for the job they had to do? Martin felt that he had so many things to worry about he didn't know which one to concentrate on. The big worry right this minute was the turkey lady and Aunt Horty fighting over Syd's lead. Hortense had taken the lead and was pulling Syd away.

"Well, then, goodbye Syd dear. I've betrayed you with my greed. And I've sold you to Americans which is even worse. You'll never forgive me." As she cried out to the dog, Hortense was pushing it into Martin's little seat. They had Dorr's convertible and the back seat was made for people one hates. Martin climbed in after Syd. It had been uncomfortable on the way down. What could he expect for the trip to Torquay? The dog climbed over him and slobbered on him and then climbed over him again trying to get out to the turkey lady.

The turkey lady chased them all the way down the driveway. "I want my Syd back. I'll call the police. You people have stolen my baby."

Hortense leaned out the window and shouted at her, "You shouldn't have cashed my check!"

Pretty soon they were out of earshot. "What if she does call the police?"

"Will you stop worrying? You sound like some old lady." His aunt mimicked him. "What if Dad finds out? What if we miss the boat? What if . . . what if . . . you are nothing but a pack of what-ifs!" Martin thought Aunt Horty must be as worried as he was. She had never chewed him out before.

Hortense hit the gas, and the road to the coast flashed by. After an hour Dorr, who'd been napping, said, "Watch out for a filling station. The car's tank is empty and mine is full."

Hortense was delighted that Dorr was awake and could take over the driving. Dorr checked the map. "We should be coming to Shrewsbury. There's bound to be a station there."

In minutes Martin spied one. "Over there. There. On your right."

"Good boy!" Martin wasn't sure if she was talking to him or to the dog. They pulled up to the gas pump.

Aunt Horty gave her orders. "Mart, take that pup for a walk. There's some grass over there. Dorr, for heaven's sake, hurry. I'll get the gas."

Martin squeezed out of the car and pulled Syd with him. He walked the dog to the grass and waited. Syd was happy to see the grass. Martin watched him. What kind of dog was this? Suddenly, he knew very well what kind of dog it was. He raced back to the car.

"Aunt Horty, you'll never believe this! We got us a girl dog. That turkey lady sold us a girl! What'll we do?" Hortense had observed the whole scene and shrugged.

Dorr came back and Hortense moved into her seat. Neither of them asked if he wasn't a bit tired of sitting sideways. "Dorr, we got us a girl dog. That crazy lady cheated us and sold us a girl."

"Oh, Martin, it doesn't make any difference. She's not to blame. We never even looked at the papers," Hortense said.

"I thought Sydney was a boy's name," Martin added defensively. "I've never met a girl called Sydney."

"We just assumed that Syd was a boy. It's our problem, but I don't think it *is* a problem. We're shipping Syd out anyway."

Dorr was pushing the little car for all it was worth. Hortense peered over at the speedometer. "Don't you think that's a little fast?"

"Well, if I don't go fast, we'll never make it to Torquay, never see the boat, and never have dinner."

Hortense leaned back and shut her eyes. Martin pushed Syd down in the seat and practically sat on her. As they got closer to the ocean, a heavy fog rolled in, covering the red MG. Martin pushed Syd's head off his lap. Syd put it right back. Martin shut his eyes. He'd had it, too.

Chapter 25

Martin chewed his fingernails. What were they ever going to do? It was still foggy and Mr. Binn wasn't about to give Hortense the keys to the *Torquay II*. They could just barely see the black fishing boat anchored out from the pier.

"Mr. Binn, you promised! We drove all the way down here." Martin pleaded, holding Syd close to his knee.

"Sorry, boy, too foggy."

"But look, the fog is already beginning to lift. By the time we get going, it will be burning off." Hortense tried to sound cheery.

"And I don't like dogs on my boats. You didn't say a word about a dog coming with you."

"This dog is a sea dog. Been sailing all his life." At that Syd squatted on a bit of dune grass. Martin froze.

Dorr looked up at the sky. The sound of a copter could be heard. "Now, Mr. Binn, if the weather is okay for airplanes, it most certainly ought to be okay for us." She tried to distract Binn. Finally, he held out the keys to

Hortense. "All right, I'll row you out. But for heaven's sake, listen for foghorns and keep tooting yours."

They pulled alongside the *Torquay II*. Dorr got on first. Martin pushed Syd up so Dorr could grab the dog by her collar. Syd put up a terrific fight.

"That's some sea dog!" Binn said sarcastically.

Hortense said, "Pull that dog up, Dorr. For heaven's sake, give it a boost, Mart."

Dorr pulled, he pushed. Syd was on board. Martin and his aunt climbed after. The boat rocked madly for a few minutes. Mr. Binn began to row off. The water was making Martin's breakfast seem unsteady. He tried to concentrate on Aunt Horty who was trying to figure out how to get the boat in gear.

"Dorr, take a look at this. It's complicated. I've never been in a boat like this before."

Dorr went to the dashboard. "It can't be all that different from a car. At that, she turned the key, got the throttle going and put the boat in gear. They literally flew past Mr. Binn, leaving him rocking in their wake. Hortense got the boat slowed down a bit, and they carefully picked their way out of the harbor and started out to sea. The caper had begun.

Chapter 26

Martin heard the horn first. "Aunt Horty, listen!"

She had heard it, too. "I think they're his foghorns."

"Do you think it's really the *Peaches?*" He looked out into the white soup that surrounded their boat.

Dorr was at the helm, Aunt Horty was navigating. "Look, Martin," she ordered, "climb out there and ink out the name on this boat. We'll be better off incognito in case we see another boat and the fog has lifted." She handed him a large, magic-marker-like-brush.

Martin looked at the bobbing prow of the *Torquay II* and wondered if he could even hang on to it. He pushed the marker into his back pocket, pulled himself up onto the rail, and carefully climbed out to the front of the boat. He leaned over and then wished he hadn't. He got back up on his knees and clung to the metal edge of the boat with one hand. With the other he began to ink out the name of the boat. It wasn't easy. His hand shook and he was scared to death he'd drop the marker into the sea. Finally, he got enough of the ink on so the name was unidentifiable. He carefully picked his way back down to the cabin.

"If this stuff is waterproof, Aunt Horty, how do we get it off?"

"I've got remover."

Leave it to her, Martin thought. She was prepared for anything.

They all heard the "eeeerrrrnk" sound again. They answered with their high pitched tooting foghorn.

Aunt Horty seemed to be brightening up. "Once we grab Clovis, we are splitting for London!" She was pacing up and down the little cabin. She didn't have much pace space. She smiled encouragingly at him. "Don't worry, Mart, we'll pull this off."

Martin tried not to worry but he kept thinking of his dad's reception that afternoon. At the rate they were going, his dad would have the Queen all to himself. They'd never make it back in time. They had to find the freighter, switch the dogs, head back to Mr. Binn's, and get to London. It was now almost nine-thirty.

Hortense held a fast meeting. "We are sitting ducks for a boat to cut us right in half in this gook. Martin, you watch the rear. I'll watch the sides, and Dorr, you keep your eyes on anything in front of us. And keep tooting the horn. Holler if you see anything. I'm going to see if I can get a reaction from that insane man by shouting at him." She went out on the prow and put her hands to her mouth. Martin didn't know how far the sound would carry, but it was a mighty shout from close by.

"Peaches, hello, Peaches, hello, Peaches, helloooooooo!"

Martin cased all the soup in back of him. Suddenly he spied something yellow. "Aunt Horty, look, there's a big yellow boat out there!"

His aunt came running. "I don't see anything yellow."

"I saw it! I saw it! A big yellow boat!"

Hortense pulled out a pair of old mother-of-pearl binoculars she'd found at Winfield House. She cleaned the lenses. She held them up, parked them firmly on her nose, and studied the whole area. What she saw made her gasp. Martin looked out. "Do you see the yellow boat?"

"No, what I see is another pair of binoculars. And they do not belong to Captain Nicholson."

Terry Tellison had heard the "eeeerrrrnk" sound several times.

Harvey Mongross, who headed up the *Geographic* expedition, looked worried. "Is that a passing freighter?"

"I certainly hope so," said Terry. But he had already registered an intuitive feeling that the sound was not from something passing. It came from something stationary. Was it possible that someone had leaked the early date? Terry didn't see how. Except for his own crew, Mongross, and the film people, no one knew about today. They had decided to come in a week early after his men had found the cache of gold ingots. As far as Terry could calculate, they had come upon a wall, knocked it down, and found trunks holding millions of dollars worth of gold. The crew knew they'd share in this booty, so they could be counted on not to talk or tip their hand about the early date. They'd stuck to the twenty-third of the month with the press as the official *Sara More* salvage day. Everything had gone like clockwork until now when they heard the "eeeerrrrnk." The thing that got to Terry most was how he had insisted that his wife come on this trip to watch. Poor Barb. She had been seasick from the second the copter had let them down on the deck of the salvager. Now she was sick as a dog and he'd put her in danger as well. She was heading over toward him, concentrating on putting one foot in front of the other. She was a pale shade of green. He put his arm around her.

"Eeeerrrrnk, eeeerrrrnk."

"What is that funny horn, Terry?"

"It's a freighter, that's all."

Then they heard a "toot, toot, toot."

"And what's that?" Barb asked.

"I'm not sure."

All three of them heard the next sound. "Yello, *Peaches,* yello."

"And *what is that?*" Barb pulled out her new binoculars. She scanned the soupy horizon. The fog was beginning to lift. For a second she glimpsed a black boat.

"Look, Terry, Harvey, look!" They all looked. "See that little black craft out there. That kind of little boat doesn't make 'eeeerrrrnk' sounds."

"What do you make of it?" Mongross whispered.

"Why two boats?" Barb asked.

Terry spilled out his fears. "I think this might be a heist. The small boat is probably armed. It's a diversion to us. While we get hooked on watching them, the big brother boat comes in for the kill. They probably have divers. And they'll kill for the kind of treasure we have down there. Harvey, tell the men to start our siren going."

Nicholson stood on the deck of the *Peaches* and watched the fog. It was burning off. By the time they hit port, it ought to be a clear day. Actually, the fog was doing him a favor, giving him great cover. He'd be able to lose the crazy ones if anything happened. Then he heard a siren. His face fell. Sirens meant trouble.

"What do you make of that siren?" Nicholson quizzed his first mate.

"Beats me. Sounds like a barge. That's quite a scream."

"Yeah, but it's not moving. It's something at anchor like we are." In a second, the fog lifted just enough for Nicholson to spot the big yellow boat. "Let's get out of here!"

"Oh, come on, Mr. Nicholson, that's nothing but a salvager. She won't bother the likes of us."

"I'm not sitting here to be trapped. Leave it to those dames to set a rendezvous in the middle of some government maneuver." He knew very well that he had chosen the rendezvous point.

"You're not even going to try to meet the ladies?"

"I'm not taking any chances. Let's get out of here."

Martin spotted the yellow boat again. "Aunt Horty, it looks like a big apartment building."

"Well, it's certainly not the *Peaches*." Aunt Horty sounded discouraged, but only for a second. "I've got an idea. Martin, whistle. Can you whistle?"

"Whistle?" Martin asked. "What for?"

"Can't you guess? If you whistle, Clovis will bark. Let's *hope* that mutt will bark. If he does we can track the *Peaches*. That creep isn't going to slip out of my hands."

Martin had noticed that the "eeeerrrrnk" sound was getting farther away.

He put his hands to his mouth and blew out a whistle that cracked the air. Within seconds he had Clovis's answer.

The *Peaches* shuddered into action like an old Caddy that hadn't been driven much. Nicholson was heading away from the rendezvous point. He heard his dog begin to bark and bay. He heard the whistle from out in front of him. They *were* out there.

His first mate yelled, "The dog is answering. You hear that. The beast hears the kid's whistle. I'll be . . . I've heard everything at sea, but never barking."

Nicholson was furious. If the dog kept barking, they'd find him, fog or no fog. "Tell that mutt to can it!" He shouted up to the men on the upper deck. "Put your arm down his choppers!"

The sailor who had Clovis on a lead wasn't about to interfere with a dog barking. He just hung on to him.

The first mate looked relieved. "Captain, I just remembered. I heard on the telly that there was some guy, an American, who was out here to pull up an old boat."

108

"Yeh, I heard that too," snarled Nicholson, "but it ain't the day for pulling it up. They're supposed to get the boat up next week." Nicholson barked out orders to head for port. Clovis barked out orders to head for Martin.

Martin hadn't calculated, nor had Dorr or Hortense, that Syd would join in the barking concert. Now there were six sounds at sea. The ever present "eeeerrrrnk", the siren, their own toot-toot-toot, his whistles, and Syd's and Clovis's bays and barks. Martin didn't know if he could whistle much more. He was running out of spit. However, he did know from experience that Clovis would bark till he fell down.

"From the sound of our dog out there, I think our trusty captain is cutting out. Isn't that just what you'd expect him to do?"

Barbara Tellison spotted the freighter. "Look, Terry, there's the 'eeeerrrrnk' boat. She's heading away from us. If they're going they must have given up the idea of robbing the site."

"I don't think so. I think they're just being smart. They'll let the little boat have at us and then they'll be back in seconds. Mongross, do you have a gun?"

Harvey Mongross looked stunned, "A gun. Yes, I do have a gun. It's a dueling pistol and it's at home."

"Terry, you've got to be kidding. Can you see who's on the little black boat?" Barbara had her binoculars pointed at the black boat.

They all looked. With the fog lifting every second, they could all see.

"There's a little boy, a huge woolly dog and two women. Surely they can't threaten this hulk," Barbara laughed.

Terry was not to be so easily taken in. "This is some new twist. Send in the children and the women to create

109

the diversion, then they'll be here in no time. Barb, I think you should go below. And stay there."

Barbara stared at him. All the green had drained away and she looked quite healthy. "Don't you think you're overdoing this just a bit? The freighter is leaving, and the only threat I can see from the black boat is a barking dog."

"Dorr, let's rev up and head for port. We'll catch that freighter."

Dorr adjusted her course, started the engine, and turned the boat around. It was a snap to follow the *Peaches* and her barking dog.

In seconds they saw the *Peaches* chugging along. And Nicholson spotted the black boat gaining on him. He gave the engineer the signal to stop the boat once again. The *Peaches* drifted a bit. It was hard for Dorr to get near enough to the freighter to establish contact without bumping against her.

The *Torquay* was close enough to the *Peaches* for a first-class shouting match.

"You idiots! Where have you been?" Nicholson yelled.

Hortense shouted back. "Listen, you lunkhead, *we're* chasing *you!*"

"You're way off course. Stupid dames!" Nicholson bellowed.

Martin caught sight of the top of Clovis's head. His heart flopped. They had made it.

"You're not only off course! You're off the wall! You were going to leave without us!" Hortense was getting hoarse from roaring.

"I stopped. I stopped. There's a big yellow boat over there. Don't you see it? You want to be see . . . n . . . ?" Nicholson's voice faded in the wind.

"We can't hear you!"

Nicholson pointed to the yellow boat. "Don't you see

that big thing? Are you blind? There are people onnnnnn itt . . .''

The fog lifted again. Aunt Horty threw up her hands in disgust. "Well, there goes what cover we did have."

They were close to the big yellow boat. It was about a city block away, but they could see it, and they knew that the yellow boat could see them.

Nicholson made the decision. He went into action. Martin watched him throw a big rope to their boat. "Catch it! Catch it, dumbbells!''

Martin caught it. "Good catch!" Dorr shouted. Martin knew that Aunt Horty was seething. Thank heavens they were on different boats. Aunt Horty would kill Nicholson if she could get her hands on him.

"Here, Mart, let me help." He and his aunt threaded the rope through a ring on the side of the boat. Then they hauled in more rope from the *Peaches*. When they had enough, Hortense climbed up on the hull and tried throwing the rope back to Nicholson. That way they'd have a working pulley.

Hortense tried three times. On her third try, Martin watched Captain Nicholson put his hands over his eyes.

"Aunt Horty, we need some weight on the end of that rope so it will carry farther." He looked around the deck. Where on earth could he find something like a brick at sea? Then he eyed the tackle box. Perfect. It had a handle, a catch, and it was made of heavy metal. Martin grabbed it, climbed up on the hull with his aunt, and pointed to the rope.

"Here, Aunt Horty, try this." They tied the rope around the metal box and threaded it through the handle.

"Do you want me to try?" Martin asked hoping to heaven she'd say no.

"No. I can do it with this." Hortense wound up like a pitcher with three men on base. She aimed and let the box fly. The weighted rope sailed high through the air and

111

landed on the deck of the *Peaches*. The crew was now all up and on deck, watching the black boat and its crew with interest.

"By Jove, she did it!" The mate was all admiration. Nicholson was thoroughly annoyed.

Now that the pulley was active for both boats, Nicholson signaled the crewman to bring on the dog. He grabbed Clovis by his chain. It took both Nicholson *and* the mate to get Clovis into the picnic basket. They slammed down the top and poked the basket's catches into place so it wouldn't open. Then they wound the rope around the basket a couple of times to keep it tight.

"Only a fruitcake would buy a picnic basket to ship a cow in," Nicholson grumbled.

They slowly let the rope out till the basket left the *Peaches*'s deck and swung down rapidly to the water and to the deck of the *Torquay II*.

"Hold her tight, idiots!" Nicholson bawled to them.

Hortense yelled back, "Pull your own weight, buster!"

"I sure hope that basket holds up," Martin worried out loud.

The basket was practically in reach when they heard a loud snap. Then another. They frantically pulled the basket in as fast as they could. Dorr tugged it to the side, and Martin and his aunt leaned over the rail and raised it into the boat. They lowered Clovis to the deck. The precious cargo had finally arrived.

Martin was down on his knees, opening the hamper. Out rolled Clovis, furious with the travel arrangement but delighted to see his master. He licked Martin's face. Martin couldn't keep from laughing.

"Oh, Aunt Horty, we did it!" He grabbed Clovis and hugged him. Syd barked with delight.

They all heard Nicholson shouting. "Send back the other pooch. I ain't got all day!"

"Mart, put Clovis down in the cabin and bring Syd."

Martin moved quickly. He grabbed Clovis, pulled him down the stairs. Sydney put up a wail. Martin hadn't counted on the dogs wanting to meet. He tried to separate them by pulling Syd away. Aunt Horty grabbed Syd and attached a purse to Syd's collar. It held Nicholson's payment for this leg of the journey. Martin shoved Clovis in the cabin. He took a deep breath and headed up. What a dismal reception this was for Clovis after a trip like the one he'd just had.

Aunt Horty was inspecting the split basket. "I think this maybe can make one more trip before it falls to pieces. Syd doesn't weigh as much as Clovis. That's a help. And I think I'll line the basket with Mr. Binn's blanket. We can put the top on and tie the blanket around the whole case. That ought to hold her."

They shoved Syd in. She put up a good fight before they hooked the lid down. Syd was off. Hortense waved. Nicholson started hauling the basket to his boat. It was a lot harder getting Syd up than it had been getting Clovis down.

"Help us, you lout!" Dorr shouted to Nicholson.

Syd finally made it to the deck of the *Peaches*. Then they watched Nicholson reach into the basket. After a second he waved Syd's collar and purse at them. Then, with horror, they watched him slip Syd back in the basket and with his knife, cut it loose. Syd fell out of the basket and into the sea. *Peaches*'s engine revved up and panted away with all the speed she had. Nicholson had the money and Mr. Binn's blanket.

"Slob! Pig! Rat!" Martin shouted. "Oh, Aunt Horty, Syd's going to die. She'll drown."

"Not while I'm alive, she won't." Hortense slipped off her sweater, sneakers, and jeans. She wound the rope around her middle, knotted it, and dived into the ocean. She had seen Syd resurface and headed toward the dog. In half a dozen long strokes, Hortense managed to reach Syd

113

and grab her by her fur. Syd was having a terrible time trying to keep her nose above water.

"Don't worry, Syd. Aunt Horty will save you!" Martin shouted.

Everyone on the salvager was lined up along the deck edge watching the freighter exchange baskets.

"What on earth?" Barbara gasped.

"What in heaven's name?" Mongross mumbled.

"They're making some kind of an exchange." Terry was still concerned about a hold up. "I'd hate to be drowning waiting for our security guard."

"Now, Terry, you're the one who kept them out. They have to come all the way from port," Mongross scolded.

Even though they could all see the action, Barbara reported it. "The big dog fell out of the basket! Oh, look! There goes one of the women. She's going in for the dog! We've got to help!"

The three of them quickly headed for the little motor launch tied to their lower deck. "I'm going," Terry said.

"I'm coming," Barbara shouted.

"I'm coming, too." Mongross hurried along with her.

Hortense shared her rope with Syd. She held the dog's chin up to keep the waves out of her face. It was a tough swim back to the boat. She could see Martin hanging over the side of the boat and Dorr trying to pull in her rope. This was the worst possible maneuver, as it kept pulling Hortense and Syd under the boat instead of next to the boat.

"Dorr, you're pulling them under. Let Aunt Horty use the rope." The *Torquay* hit a wave and turned about. Dorr let go of the rope. Aunt Horty disappeared. Martin moved fast; he was a good swimmer. He pulled his shoes off and jumped in. The cold water hit him like a ton of bricks. He sank at once, below the surface. As Hortense surfaced, pulling Syd with her, Martin's head disappeared.

"Martin Prentiss," she screamed at him, "get out of this water immediately!" Martin heard her as his head came up for air. He pushed his legs and feet as hard as he could to get going. He had never been in the ocean when the swell was as big as this one. Walking into the waves from the beach was an entirely different affair from plopping down into deep water. They both reached the boat at the same time. He helped his aunt push Syd up. Syd was dead weight. Dorr grabbed the dog by the nape of her neck, held on for dear life, and tried to avoid Syd's kicks. Finally she pulled the dog onto *Torquay II*'s deck. Dorr untied the rope on Syd and threw it overboard. Aunt Horty caught it, then she grabbed Martin by his shirt and gave him one big shove into Dorr's arms.

Martin and Syd sat on the deck exhausted. Dorr figured that if Hortense had the rope around her she could use the pulley idea and simply pull her in. In seconds, she had lifted Hortense high into the air—sideways. When Martin saw his aunt hanging in the air, he looked at Dorr. They both began to giggle. Aunt Horty did not think this was funny. "Put me down, Dorr, for the love of heaven. It's not funny. I'm freezing."

Dorr let the rope go and Hortense hit the water again. Martin and Dorr were both laughing so hard they were helpless. Finally his aunt pulled herself over the side. She fell onto the deck and just moaned.

"Are you all right?" Martin asked, trying to keep from laughing again.

His aunt was furious. "No thanks to you two buffoons."

Martin felt guilty. "I'm sorry, Aunt Horty. I didn't mean to laugh at you. It's just when you were hanging up there we couldn't help it." His teeth were chattering and he tried to keep warm by slapping his arms at his sides.

Dorr pulled off her sweater and handed it to Martin,

then got Aunt Horty's stuff from the bench. "Here, Martin, put this on. Here, Horty, pull on your sweater. You'll both die of cold if you don't." Hortense slipped on her sweater and tried to pull her jeans over her wet underwear. They were so busy they never even saw the little launch pull up next to their boat. "Ahoy there," shouted Terry.

Hortense gasped and kept trying to stand up with her jeans stuck in the middle of her legs.

Martin took a deep breath. This was it. The police. No question. Syd seemed delighted and kept shaking her wet hair at the company. She was the only warm reception the motor boat crowd got.

"You all okay?" Terry shouted.

By this time the boats were bobbing next to each other. It didn't seem to matter they were so close, everyone shouted anyway.

"Oh, yes, yes. We just had a spill," Hortense roared.

"Dog overboard." Martin used his hands at his mouth to make his sentence heard.

"What are you doing out here?" Terry yelled. "This is off-limits territory. Didn't you see the markers? And what was that freighter you were roped to?"

"Oh, the freighter." Aunt Horty's face reddened. "That's my brother's freighter. We bring him mail and clothes and sometimes a picnic lunch." Hortense looked at Dorr and Martin. She was embarrassed over this lie.

"What do you call that? Chicken in the basket?" Barbara yelled over to them, laughing.

Their story was so unbelievable that Terry laughed, too. "Why don't you take it to him in port?"

"Take all the fun out of it. It's a family custom."

On that note, Dorr decided to rev up the *Torquay*. She pulled up anchor and zipped off as fast as she could. They all waved at the launch. "Goodbye, goodbye, thanks for the help."

"Thanks for coming to our rescue," Martin called back.

116

The motor launch turned around and headed back to their big boat. They hadn't gotten near it when the police boats finally arrived. The police didn't want to hear anything from them. They definitely wanted to arrest Barbara, Terry and Mongross.

By the time Terry made it clear that *they* were the ones who had called them, the black boat with the dog, two women, and a little boy had gone. The freighter was also far off in the distance.

Aunt Horty gave a deep sigh of relief as the police sirens got farther away from them and finally stopped.

"Wouldn't you know it? Now that we could use the fog, it's nothing but mist." Hortense pulled a bottle of oil from her case and a rag and handed it all to Martin. "Get out there, baby, and clean up the name. We're heading home."

Chapter 27

Martin figured that nothing else bad could possibly happen. He hopped out on to the hull, scrunched down and put something that smelled of bananas on the cloth. He scrubbed back the name of the boat. By the time he got back, Hortense had packed all the rods and reels and was packing up her case and Dorr's.

"I hope Mr. Binn doesn't give me a bad time over his blanket."

Syd had calmed down and was sitting up on the bench enjoying the breezes. Her hair blew every which way. Dorr was really slicing through the water. They all knew what time it was. Eleven-thirty.

"I don't know why everyone is in such a bad mood. I think we accomplished our mission," Aunt Horty said proudly.

"I'll say we did. We more than accomplished our mission." Dorr steered the boat toward the shore. "We now have *two* dogs to smuggle into England. Got some thoughts about how to tell the ambassador this?"

Martin drew in his breath. This was going to be some

problem. "We can tell him the turkey lady gave us two-fers."

"I don't picture him buying that line." Dorr laughed.

"I'm going to get Clovis out, Aunt Horty, he's been locked up ever since we got him."

"Just leave him where he is, honey. We don't need two wild animals on this deck. I have to figure a way to get us by Binn." She leaned over the rail and ran her fingers through her wet hair, trying to dry it.

"Okay," Dorr said, "let me try this on you. How about Martin getting off at the pier with Syd? He can race past Mr. Binn's office. He won't stop till he gets to our car. Then he'll be out of sight of Binn's pier. I'll go next and take Clovis. I'll stop and tell Mr. Binn that Martin is sick. Horty, you take the boat back into the harbor and dock it. I'll see that Mr. Binn goes to get you. That will take his mind off us."

They were coming into the harbor. "Here, Martin. Put your shoes on and your shorts." His aunt pulled them off the flag pole where they'd been hanging to dry. Martin pulled them on. "Yuk, they feel terrible and they're ice-cold."

"Wait till you get your shirt."

Dorr cut the motor down to an idle and carefully slipped next to the pier. Hortense took over. Martin hopped out. He had Syd on one piece of the rope; the other piece was saved for Clovis. "Okay, Martin, go!"

He raced down the pier toward Mr. Binn's office. Syd tripped and fell as she ran. Martin could only think of one way to describe Syd. A mess. He sped past Mr. Binn's office. He noticed that Mr. Binn was reading his paper. He got to the steps and pulled Syd up with him. Syd did not want to go up the steps. Just as Martin and the dog disappeared from Mr. Binn's surprised stare, Dorr came running with Clovis. She shouted to Mr. Binn as she flew by his doorway, "Martin is sick. Will you go get Ms.

119

Morley? She's anchoring the boat. Thank you." Her voice got fainter as she headed up the steps.

Mr. Binn stood up and peered out at Dorr's receding figure. He watched her try to get up the steps. Her dog decided not to go up the steps. Instead the dog made an emergency stop and lifted his leg. Dorr tried to pull him along anyway. "Downright cruel," mumbled Mr. Binn.

He then ambled back to his office and went past it down to the end of the pier where he kept his rowing boat. He kept nudging an idea around in his head. Were there two dogs? Or just one dog? Seemed to him that there were two dogs. Didn't the young fellow have a dog, too? Funny. He could swear there were two dogs, yet, there had only been one dog on the way out. Mighty funny, he thought.

He rowed out to the *Torquay*. Hortense smiled down at him. "Here, Mr. Binn, just give me a hand with this stuff." She handed down the rods, reels, and her bag. Then she slipped over the rail and with no effort slid into his boat. He saw that her hair was all wet.

"Took a little swim while I was out there," Hortense tried to explain Mr. Binn's stare. "Water was cold but refreshing."

"Where's your tackle box?"

"That's really why I went for a swim. It fell over."

"That all that went over?"

"And your blanket. I'll make it good."

"You have to pay for it. I don't want just any old blanket."

"So," said Hortense pleasantly. "We didn't catch anything but a cold."

Binn pulled up to the pier and grabbed hold of it. Hortense slipped out of the boat and climbed on to the pier. They walked back to his office. He returned her deposit less the cost of a new blanket. She gave him the keys to the boat.

"You were a dear to let us have the boat today. It would

120

have been so disappointing to Martin. He'd counted on fishing for such a long time."

"Didn't do him any good. He's sick so I hear."

Hortense looked surprised. "Oh, yes, of course, he's sick."

"Well, you should have listened to me. No day for sailin' or fishin'."

"We'll come back." She pumped his hand up and down and then lit off for the steps as fast as the other two had.

Binn watched her go. He plopped the keys for the *Torquay* into his desk drawer and locked it. Then he locked up the office. No other boat was out. He might as well go home. He walked to the steps and stopped.

"There is something fishy about that crowd. Mighty fishy."

Chapter 28

Martin had been uncomfortable in the back seat with only Syd. With Clovis *and* Syd it was torture. Both dogs smelled.

"It just stinks back there," Dorr moaned. "Stinks!" She looked in the rearview mirror. "You should just see the three of you. It's a picture."

"I don't care how it smells. I've got Clovis back." He hugged the huge beast.

"It *still* smells," Hortense complained.

"You thought this plan up, Aunt Horty. Remember?"

"You two helped."

"You paid for it," Dorr added.

"We'll all pay for it if we don't get flying."

They had left at one o'clock almost on the dot. That gave them three hours to cover the country roads and buck London traffic. It wasn't a lot of time.

Hortense turned back to Martin. "I don't know about you, Mart, but I've never had such a wild time. Life on the chimp farm is a breeze compared with life at sea with Captain Nicholson."

Dorr put down the convertible top. "There, maybe that will help the smell and dry the beasts. Here, Martin," she grabbed a hairbrush from her case on the floor, "when you get a chance, try to brush their hair so they won't look so bedraggled when we get home."

"You've got to be kidding," Martin said sarcastically. "I can't even move my arms."

Hortense's hair was flying, Dorr's was flying, the dogs' hair was flying. "We look like a moving beauty salon," Martin said. He wondered if his shorts would ever dry. Finally, Clovis got sick of the drying system and settled his head on Martin's lap. For a brief second Martin shut his eyes.

"There were no detours when we came by yesterday," Dorr moaned. Martin sat up. There was a long line of cars waiting for the flag-man to give them the go-ahead. Hortense got nervous. "Just go around the line."

"Are you crazy?" Dorr looked at her. "I don't want a ticket today. We haven't got time for a ticket."

"I don't mean go in the wrong lane, I mean go through the field. It looks fairly even."

Dorr reversed as much as she could and headed toward the field. Martin couldn't believe she was doing this.

"Okay, everyone, hang on!"

Martin not only had to hang on to keep from being thrown from the car, but he had to hang on to Clovis and Syd as well.

"For Pete's sake, Dorr, go slow! I can't hang on to everything back here."

Dorr slowed down and they bumped along the meadow. Within a few minutes they came out where the other flag-signal man was hidden.

"Hey, *wait there just a minute!*" The flag man shouted at them. But Dorr had cleared the detour and they sped off down the road.

"What time is it?"

"One-thirty," Hortense yelled over the wind.

They were still out on country roads. They were nowhere near London.

Martin watched his aunt begin to look worried. Then she really got edgy when they hit the city. There was a lot of traffic. "Even if we can get to the house before four, we can't meet the Queen looking this piggy."

Dorr smiled smugly. "I called Sydney while we were waiting for you to settle with Mr. Binn. I swore him to secrecy. He's getting all our clothes down to the spare rooms in the back of the house. We can go in the back way, dump the dogs with the gardener, and get showered and dressed in minutes."

Hortense relaxed a mite.

Martin saw the one-way arrow. Dorr didn't. She was trying to cut over to another street. Unfortunately, the one she chose to cut to was also one-way. Martin shut his eyes. He heard his second siren of the day.

It was the police siren, and it was right behind them. They had flashing lights, the works. What if they confiscated Clovis?

"Dorr, you'd better stop." Martin pushed his face in between Dorr and Aunt Hortense. *"Stop!"*

"We haven't got time to stop. If we can just make it to the house, we'll be okay. Don't we have amnesty or something?"

"You mean immunity?" Hortense laughed. "No, we do *not!* And if you don't stop, we'll end up in jail. Now STOP!"

Dorr did a wild U-turn. They passed the police car. They were now going the right way. The police were breaking the law. Dorr turned right onto a major thoroughfare. She was trying to lose the cops in traffic. Martin thought this was funny and laughed.

"Dorr, we can't lose them. This car stands out like a moon vessel. How about flying?"

"We're already doing that," Hortense said sarcastically.

The police had gone round the block and were back on their tail. Big Ben chimed 3:45. Dorr sighed and pulled over.

A tall, red-faced policeman approached the car. He hung over Dorr's little car. "Well now, madam, may I ask where you are going at such speed? And on a one-way street, to boot?"

Martin piped up. "To see the Queen!"

The cop smiled. "You know, I hear that one quite often. I'll have your papers, please."

Martin did the talking. "Honest, officer, that's exactly where we are going. My dad is having the Queen for tea."

It sounded like the ambassador was going to sandwich her between white bread. "We just have to get there."

The officer handed the papers back to Dorr. "Wait here a minute." He strode back to his car to talk with his partner.

"They *say* that they are trying to get to Winfield House to meet the Queen. What should I do?"

"What's the lady's name?"

"Prentiss. The little boy is quite upset."

"Prentiss. Prentiss. Sounds familiar. Tell you what we can do. We'll give them speeding tickets and lead them home. If they're telling the truth, we'll let them go. If not, well, I guess we'll run them in."

Chapter 29

Prentiss paced back and forth. "Did you ring the turkey lady, Sydney?" he questioned his assistant.

"Yes, sir. She wants her dog back. Seems the dog's name is Sydney and I was quite confused."

"Why did I let them out of my sight?"

"I'm sure they'll be here. Ms. Hortense is always prompt." He couldn't tell the ambassador that he'd talked to Dorr and knew they would be back.

"I am going to kill Ms. Hortense."

"Yes, sir."

"I am going to throttle Dorr Prentiss."

"Ms. Hortense would never miss a party like this. Not for anything."

"I hope you're right. Oh, oh, here come the limos." The ambassador and Sydney headed for the front portico where they would meet the Queen. He knew she'd be conveniently late so that everyone could be in place when she arrived. Everyone except his family.

Chapter 30

The police escort was the best thing that could have happened. Both cars turned into the drive at 4:10. The gatekeeper hurried out and pushed open the gates. Dorr shrugged at the cops. They waved her on. The gatekeeper's greeting was enough proof for the London police.

Dorr streaked down the main drive, then headed for the back of the house. Hortense gave Martin a signal to get the dog ropes ready. She hurried both the dogs over to the gardener who was all dressed up for the big event. He'd get a view of the Queen from the kitchen. He really didn't want two dirty, hairy beasts thrust at him now, but he took the ropes and pulled the dogs away.

"Keep them locked up," Aunt Horty advised him. "They're incorrigible. Then, if you would please let the ambassador know that we're here."

They flew into the back rooms. Their clothes were all laid out for them. Martin went to his room, Hortense and Dorr shared. Martin looked at his watch. They'd even have time for a shower. He grabbed his velvet blazer, silk shirt, and trousers and headed for the spare bath. Two of the maids were helping Dorr and Hortense. He was on his own.

He was finished first and headed out to the front of the house weaving in and out of special salons and living rooms. He peeked out the French doors. His dad was standing with Sydney and a whole coterie of people on the low front steps. There were baskets of flowers everywhere. A white limo silently crept up the drive. Martin slipped out and found his way to his dad's side.

"Hi, Dad, did you think we weren't coming?"

The ambassador gave Martin a fast inspection. He passed. Then just before the limo drew up, Dorr joined him on his other side. He turned around. He knew Hortense was there. He recognized her perfume.

She whispered, "I thought you said you were having a party. Looks to me like everyone is just standing around."

With all the action of chauffeurs and aides at the door of the limo, the ambassador had time for only one sentence. He whispered back to Hortense. "I'm going to get you for this."

He walked to the car to greet the Queen.

She wore a pale blue, perfectly cut silk coat over a matching flowered tea dress. With it, of course, she wore a pale blue straw toque. She wore gloves and carried a small purse on her arm. She accepted champagne but didn't drink it. She chose a tea sandwich but it sat on her plate. The ambassador seated her in the main salon in a large Queen-like chair. She had a view of the Winfield gardens. The roses were quite magnificent, and the Queen told John Prentiss she was properly impressed.

Martin was anxious to tell her that he liked England. "Have you ever been to Torquay?"

"Oh, indeed I have," said the Queen.

"Did you know that Napoleon was a prisoner there?"

Of course she knew but she didn't let Martin know she knew. "You don't mean it!"

128

Hortense curtsied although she had sworn that *she* wasn't bowing to anyone. There was just something about this enormously courteous warm woman that brought out respect in everyone.

Ambassador Prentiss stood up and faced the Queen. People gathered around on cue.

"Your Majesty, thank you for coming here today. The United States and Britain have shared so much history we wanted to share a bit more. Next week, an American will make history by raising a British ship, the *Sara More,* and returning all its treasures to England where they belong.

"I had hoped that Mr. Tellison would be with us today to present this gift to you in person. But he's off the coast of Torquay getting ready for the big day next week."

At the word Torquay, the Queen looked a bit quizzical. It was the second time Torquay had been mentioned in fifteen minutes.

"One of the most precious items Mr. Tellison found was this emerald," the ambassador continued, "and one of England's finest gem dealers said it was, without doubt, one of the most beautiful stones he had ever seen." He gave the Queen one of his charming smiles. "I might add that he made a very good offer for the gem. We hope that this emerald will become part of the crown jewel collection and be labeled *A gift from the Sara More*.

He handed her a satin box and she opened it. Then she turned the box around so that everyone would get a glimpse of the green sparkle of the emerald. Martin thought it was very much like a robin's egg he once held, only this was a green robin.

The crowd applauded. "Ah! Oh! Beautiful, well done, bravo!"

Just as the Queen was about to respond to the ambassador's gift there was an uproar from the outside terrace. It came from the people who had listened to the presentation from the garden terrace. People pointed, laughed, and

129

clapped some more. The Queen craned her neck to see what on earth was going on.

Martin couldn't believe what he saw. There was an eruption of white, gray, and darker gray fur from the rosebushes. Sydney and Clovis barked, bayed, yipped, and raced about the yard.

His dad's whole body stiffened and his face began to turn red. Martin decided that the time was right to get those dogs out of the party. He raced after the pair. He was able to grab Syd, who wasn't half as agile as Clovis in a race. Martin handed Syd over to the gardner, who was huffing and puffing and mumbling excuses for their appearance in the garden. Then Martin went for Clovis, who, deprived of Syd, was determined to meet the Queen.

The crowd parted. The Queen sat up straight to watch. She caught sight of Clovis and watched the ambassador's son grab the other sheepdog and hand him to a servant. She laughed. This put everyone but the ambassador at ease. Ordinarily, dogs did not attend Queen's tea parties.

"Why, Ambassador Prentiss, no one mentioned to me that you were a sheepdog fancier. My, they are frisky!"

Clovis had one target in mind. He wanted to say hello to his favorite person in the world. Martin saw him heading for his dad. The ambassador quickly stepped to the far right and Clovis decided to head for the Queen.

Martin said loudly, "Oh, no you don't!" He made a charge for the dog. Everyone gasped as Martin did a turn about and ran interference.

"Sit. Sit. Clovis. Sit!" Clovis sat. He not only sat, he pulled off a trick no one knew he could do. He positioned himself directly in front of the Queen and with his rump in the air, put his forelegs down. It looked, no matter how many people said later that it most certainly could never have been, just like he was bowing to the Queen.

"Oh, my dear, how absolutely marvelous!" She reached over and petted Clovis's top-knot. Everyone clapped. Clovis was so delighted he moved up to put his slobbering chin right in the royal lap. Martin grabbed several napkins from the table and got to the Queen before Clovis's chin did. The Queen smiled and bestowed another gloved pat on Clovis's white-gray head. Clovis was really home at last.

Chapter 31

Martin watched the last of the limos slide down the drive past the gates. He saw his father go limp and give a huge sigh of relief. Then the ambassador turned to Martin and Dorr and Aunt Horty.

"I would like to ask you all one question. That big dog, the one who kow-towed to the Queen. That *is* who I think it is, isn't it?"

"Isn't *who,* Dad?"

"You know good and well 'who.' "

Martin thought he might as well own up. There was no way to mistake Clovis. "You're right, Dad. That is who you think it is. It's Clovis. Sydney was a decoy."

The ambassador looked at Hortense. "I don't want to hear about it. I don't want to understand anything. I don't need to know."

Martin felt relieved. "In that case, Dad, I'm going to get a sandwich. I'm starved. You always serve such ukky stuff at your parties. And then, Dad, if it's okay with you, I'm going to turn in. I've had some day."

"I'll just bet you have." The ambassador watched his tall, gangly son leave the room.

Dorr gave her Dad a kiss. "Wait, Mart, I'll go with you. Let's get Clovis and Syd." The dogs had been exiled from the party after Clovis bowed.

Martin and Dorr shared a sandwich. From Dorr's room they could look down on the garden, and they both watched their Dad and Aunt Horty sit down on a bench. Martin did a double take when he saw his dad put his arm around Hortense's shoulders. He looked at Dorr.

"Know what I think?"

"No, what do you think?"

"I think Dad's in love with Aunt Horty."

"And I think Horty is nuts about Dad."

"That would be nice. She could live with us all the time. Hey, Dorr, she'd be your second stepmother." He grinned mischievously.

"I'm too old for a stepmother, but if I had to have one, I'd sure pick Horty."

"I just love her, Dorr. She's so like Mom. Do you think she'd really marry Dad?"

"I suspect she just might do that, Martin." They continued to stare down at Hortense and John Prentiss. Finally, Dorr turned Martin toward the door of her suite. She gave him a push. "Come on, Martin, let's give them a little privacy."

"Oh, Dorr. It's just getting good."

Chapter 32

Barbara and Terry were having breakfast in Portsmouth. They had decided to stay on in Portsmouth for a couple of days, then hit London for some theatre, and return for the big day. Mongross had gone right on to London. He'd be back for the big day, too.

"This time the *Sara* comes up instead of my breakfast." Barbara laughed. She was looking at a photo in the London *Times* of her and Terry on the yellow salvager.

"I can hardly wait to see her afloat again. What a beautiful ship." Terry mused. Then he saw Barbara poring over another photo in the paper. "What's that?"

"I don't believe it! Wait till you get a gander at this!" She handed the paper to him.

"It's Prentiss and the Queen."

"I know. He had his reception yesterday. I wonder if the Queen liked the emerald?"

"Look at the line-up behind him, Terry. Look." She pointed at the picture.

Terry studied the photo for a second time. Then his mouth dropped open. "It's . . . it's . . . it's *them*. The loons from the black boat delivering lunch."

"Precisely! That kid is Prentiss's son. The younger woman," she pointed to the type under the photo, "is his daughter. And the tall one is his sister-in-law, the famous anthropologist, Hortense Morley. Now what do you make of *that*?"

"What on earth do you think was going on yesterday?" Terry studied the picture. "How did they manage to get to London for the party? They must have gone by air. You know, Barb, there's a lot more to know about this. A lot more."

Mr. Binn sipped his tea and perused the morning papers. He had just turned the page when he took a deep breath and pointed out the picture to his wife.

"Why, it's the Queen, dear," Mrs. Binn said.

"I *know* that!" Binn was irritated.

"She's a real get-abouter."

Binn pointed to the picture. "See those folks behind her and the ambassador from America? Those are the same people, Emma, who rented my boat yesterday. The very same ones I told you about. The ones with the dog. Imagine, they're from the ambassador's family."

And once again Binn had that unsettling feeling that there was something very wrong about yesterday.

"I think," Binn said firmly, "that there is a lot more to know about yesterday than *I* know."

Nicholson drank his beer in one gulp. He sat at the bar. He was furious. That dame had ratted on him and he'd been hauled in by customs. They'd had him for hours. They practically tore up the boat. The crew was quarantined and they were mad.

"It was probably the dog," his mate said. "You should never have cut him down and let him drown. That wasn't right."

"Oh, shut up. It would have been just great to have had

that pooch on board with customs. We'd all be in the hoosegow.''

He leafed through the paper. He stopped on one page and pulled the whole sheet of paper toward him for very close inspection. He saw the picture of the Queen. He saw Dorr. He saw the red-headed dame, he saw the kid. They looked happy. They probably had saved the dog. Maybe he could blackmail the lot of them.

"I should. She still owes me ten percent. And she wouldn't want the ambassador of the Yewnited States to hear about dogs coming into England, would she? Imagine me and the *Peaches* working for such as the Ambassador of the Yewnited States?''

"If I was you, Captain, I'd just leave well enough alone.''

"Well.'' The Captain finished up his beer and ordered another. "Well, all I got to say is that there's a lot more to know here.''

Mrs. Grant answered the phone in the kitchen. She was just on her way out. She stopped in every day to check out the house and she was lucky she had just popped in when the phone rang. It was Martin.

"Martin! What happened? Did you get Clovie? You did? That's wonderful! What? You don't want me to pick up the new pooch? Why not? You're going to write me. All right. How's everyone? Your dad? Ms. Hortense? Ms. Dorr? Me? I'm fine, just fine. I miss you, too. I was glad to do it, Martin. Glad. Okay. Thanks for calling, honey. Give my love to everyone.''

She hung up and plopped down on one of the kitchen chairs. "Well, I'll be. They kept both the doggies. Wonder what happened? Guess there's a lot more to know about this situation.''

Hortense, Dorr, and Martin were having a late breakfast. Dorr was trying to work a crossword puzzle. Martin

136

sipped his chocolate and studied Dorr's paper upside down. It always seemed to him that other people's papers were more interesting, especially if you had to look at them upside down.

"Dorr"—Martin grabbed for the paper—"can I have a look at that?"

"What's the magic word, Martin?" Aunt Horty chided.

"Please, Aunt Horty. No, please, Dorr."

Dorr gave him the paper and he turned it around. "Look, Aunt Horty." He pointed to a picture at the top of the page.

They all studied the photo.

Martin read, "Portsmouth. Yesterday, hundreds of gold ingots and legendary gems were hauled to the surface of the ocean waters from the bottom of the sea. It was all part of the famous *Sara More* treasure." The photo showed guards loading a security truck. "There's Mr. Tellison and that must be his wife." Martin tried to sound cool. He wasn't. "They're the people in the little boat! And they're the people from the big yellow boat," he shouted.

"Good heavens!" Aunt Horty said. "So that's what happened yesterday."

Martin's dad came in the room and helped himself to Aunt Horty's coffee. "Did you see this, John?" Aunt Horty handed him the paper.

"Yes, I did. I saw it earlier."

"How did you get the emerald, Dad, if it didn't come up till yesterday?"

"Terry brought it from the ship last week. He knew I was searching for a gift for the Queen. I really think she was impressed, don't you?"

Everyone thought she was *very* impressed.

"Did you tell them, Hortense?" Martin's dad seemed anxious.

"No, we've just had too many other things to think about."

137

"Well, tell them." He stood right by Aunt Horty.

Aunt Horty looked at Martin. "Martin, I . . . I . . . your father . . . and I . . ."

Martin grinned. "I know. You're going to get married."

"How did you know?" Prentiss asked. "You *did* tell them, Hortense."

"I most certainly *did not* tell them. How *did* you know?"

Martin and Dorr just laughed. "What I want to know, Aunt Horty . . ." Martin went to her. She gave him a hug—so hard he had to come up for air. "What I want to know is, will you bring Philippa into England?"

"No," his aunt said firmly. "No, Martin, no way. I am simply not up to that."

"Me neither," his sister said positively.

"Ridiculous idea." His dad smiled. "Everyone knows that you absolutely cannot bring a pet into England."

They laughed so hard they woke up Syd. But Clovis continued to snore. He was exhausted from yesterday.

For all intents and purposes, the Clovis caper ended on a beautiful day in June in England. It ended in a small, charming, bed-breakfast dining room in Portsmouth. It ended in Torquay. It ended on the *S.S. Peaches*. The boat was temporarily quarantined and the crew had a fit over their confinement. And it ended happily at Winfield House in London for Martin Prentiss. His aunt was going to live with them full-time. And Clovis was home for good.